MW00769795

INVASION: ZOMBIE APOCALYPSE

THEM POST-APOCALYPTIC SERIES BOOK ONE

M.D. MASSEY

MODERN DIGITAL PUBLISHING, AUSTIN, TX

FREE BOOK OFFER!
Get your FREE novella now at
MDMassey.com

Modern Digital Publishing
P.O. Box 682
Dripping Springs, Texas 78620

THEM Book Zero: Invasion/ M.D. Massey. — 1st ed.

Dedicated to all the warriors who are still fighting their own personal battles, day by day.

"While my wife at my side lies slumbering, and the wars are over long,
And my head on the pillow rests at home, and the vacant midnight passes,
And through the stillness, through the dark, I hear, just hear, the breath of my infant,
There in the room, as I wake from sleep, this vision presses upon me:
The engagement opens there and then, in fantasy unreal;
The skirmishers begin—they crawl cautiously ahead—
   I hear the irregular snap! snap!
I hear the sounds of the different missiles—the short t-h-t! t-h-t! of the rifle balls;
I see the shells exploding, leaving small white clouds—
   I hear the great shells shrieking as they pass;
The grape, like the hum and whirr of wind through the trees,
   (quick, tumultuous, now the contest rages!)
All the scenes at the batteries themselves rise in detail before me again..."

WAKE

I WAS JUST PULLING my old Toyota Hilux 4x4 into the Stop N' Steal parking lot when I saw him standing there, kinda swaying back and forth, just generally waiting to get run over. *Aw shit*, I thought. *Better help him before Randy comes along and locks him up.* Randy was the local constable, and along with the sheriff's deputies who patrolled this area, he was most of what passed for the law in these parts.

Folks who aren't from Texas don't realize it, but there are counties in West Texas bigger than most Yankee states. Most of them are sparsely populated, which means there's a whole lot of land with not a lot of law to go around. Suits me just fine. I like to spend my time with as little government interference as possible.

Another thing most folks don't realize is just how close most of the state is to Mexico. That means we get a lot of illegals coming up from south of us, looking for work and a better life. I don't hold it against them, being as my ancestors pretty much came to Texas the same way, albeit before Texas was a state. Even though I'm mostly a fan of respecting the rule of law, I still try to help them any way I can.

Sadly, this character looked like he'd been sick for days. Nearest hospital was in Kerrville, and he likely had no way to get there, all on his own. Musta just got into town. Coyotes would smuggle illegals just far enough to evade border patrol, then they'd give them a jug of water and say, "Walk that way until you find a town." A lot of them died each year, lost in the desert scrub—most often from dehydration, starvation, or exposure. A good part of them were kids. I had an uncle who'd worked as a cop on the border in South Texas for the better part of 50 years, and he'd tell stories about finding kids dead in the scrub. Haunted him for the rest of his days.

So when I see a guy like this one, I do my best to step in and help them get where they need to be. But this guy, he looked like he was really bad off. For one, he stuck out like a sore thumb, which was bound to get him picked up by *La Migra* quick. He was wearing a pair of snakeskin boots that looked like the soles were worn right through, a pair of acid-washed jeans that had seen better days way back in the eighties when they were probably made, and a dime store western shirt. An Astros hat topped it all off, which he'd probably bought thinking it would help him blend in, the poor guy. I pulled my truck up and yelled out the window to him.

"¡Oye! ¿Necesita un paseo?" *Hey! Do you need a ride somewhere?* Nothing. The guy just stood there, rocking back and forth. I could see his eyes were glazed over, and he looked like he was about to pass out. I grabbed a water bottle from the passenger seat, turned the truck off, and got out to help him.

"¿Señor, quieres agua?" I asked as I approached him from the front.

He was still zoning out as I walked up. It looked like he'd need medical assistance, for sure. I unscrewed the cap and walked up with the bottle held out to him; just as I did, his eyes rolled back and he collapsed.

"Shit!"

I dropped to the ground next to him and shifted into combat lifesaver mode. The guy looked like he was either vomiting or foaming at the mouth, so I rolled him over onto his side and checked to make sure his airway was clear. A few years in 3rd Batt and a couple of tours in Afghanistan, and you pick up a few things about first aid. He appeared to be breathing okay, so I looked around to find someone to call 9-1-1.

Thankfully by this time we'd started to gather a crowd, mostly tourists who were down here to see the leaves turn at Lost Maples State Park and maybe do a little tubing on the Frio, what with the Indian summer we were having. I tolerated them most days, but just barely. Bunch of yuppies and hipsters from Austin, with the occasional drunk-ass frat boy thrown in for good measure. I kept reminding myself they'd be gone in a few weeks, and good riddance. I also reminded myself that frat boys often brought sorority girls with them, which tended to make the summer and fall tourist seasons a bit more bearable. If only just.

Most of them had their cell phones out and appeared to be filming the action. Welcome to the age of social media, where idiots would rather shoot a viral video than help their fellow humans. Sign of the times, I suppose. I didn't even own a cell phone, refused to carry one. Like I wanted the government to be able to track my every move. They had gotten enough out of me in Afghanistan; now I just wanted to be left alone.

I turned to a fat guy in a Hawaiian print shirt, flip flops, and cargo shorts. "You, Peter Griffin! Call 9-1-1, this guy obviously needs help."

The guy gave me a hurt look and started dialing his phone. "I was going to call...no need to start insulting people," he mumbled as he dialed.

I sneered and went back to helping my anonymous friend. In the time it had taken to tell the fat guy to call an ambulance, the guy had stopped breathing.

"Aw, hell!" I said to no one in particular. I jumped up and pushed through the crowd to my truck and pulled a med kit from behind the seat. It had a CPR pocket mask in it, because damned if I was going to give this guy mouth to mouth through all that foam and puke. I got it ready as I pushed my way back through the crowd, and of course no one else had started CPR yet. I dropped down next to the guy and cleared his airway again, giving him two quick breaths, then I started chest compressions. I could hear the crowd mumbling behind me as I worked.

"Oh man, this is going up on Facebook right now! The guys are going to flip!"

"Ew, he threw up in his mouth. Gross. I bet he stinks, too."

"Shouldn't someone call an ambulance? I think they did already, right?"

"Where's the Border Patrol when you need 'em? If they were doing their cotton pickin' jobs, this kind of thing'd never happen."

And so on. I blocked them out and focused on keeping this guy's heart beating for him, a task that seemed to drag on into eternity. It was always like that when you were pumping on somebody's chest, which I'd done more times than I would have liked in Afghanistan. As I looked down at my hands, willing the guy's chest up and down, I could almost smell the gunpowder and feel the grit between my teeth. To my horror, before I'd made it through two cycles of compressions I started to feel like I was back *there* again.

Oh, bloody hell. Not again. My breathing started to quicken and I could feel a full-on panic attack about to hit. *Not good, Sully. Not good at all.*

I tried to slow my breathing, which was kind of difficult considering all the work that went into keeping the guy's blood moving and keeping air going in and out of his lungs. So far no one had volunteered to do two-person CPR with me, and I was getting light-headed along with feeling like my own heart was beating out of my chest. Everything closed in. I couldn't focus. Couldn't breathe. Couldn't think.

Just a few more minutes. Surely just a few more minutes. Ambulance should be here anytime now, I reassured myself. Only, it might not. Real County covered over 700 square miles, and the local EMS crews could be busy with a drowning, agricultural accident, or motor vehicle collision halfway across the county. Just thinking about that started making me flip out more.

"Balls!" I whispered loudly in frustration. I was starting to see spots, my breathing was coming fast and shallow, and I was about to lose my shit. That's about the time the guy came back to life.

————

I WAS PUMPING AWAY on the guy's chest when his eyes popped open. They were rheumy and covered in a white haze, not unlike someone who had suffered flash burns to the eyes. His eyeballs sort of rolled around a bit, then he took in a deep, shuddering breath, starting to moan and paw at the air and ground.

I placed a hand on his shoulder to calm him. "Cálmate hombre, todo está bien. La ayuda ya viene en camino." *Calm down, everything is fine and help is on the way.*

His eyes rolled around again and centered on me. He paused, and I thought I'd finally gotten through to him. Then, he lunged up at me with lightning speed, bowling me over and landing on top of me. Out of habit, I pulled him in between my legs into the jiu-jitsu guard position and got a forearm under his chin.

Unfortunately, he had already grabbed me by the neck with both hands. He pulled my face toward his with such force I thought he might snap my neck.

In a split second his face was just inches from mine. He snapped his teeth at me in a pecking manner, bobbing his head forward and apparently trying to take a bite out of my face. The scary thing was, despite having years of Modern Army Combatives training, I couldn't move his hands off my neck. He was *that* strong. I'm not a small man, but in all my years in the military sparring with guys my size and bigger, I'd never grappled with someone who had this much raw strength.

He's on drugs, I thought. *Great.* I was already freaking out from the panic attack that had come on just moments earlier, and the spots in my vision were getting larger. I knew it would only be seconds before I blacked out, and none of the bystanders were moving to help. I looked around frantically for assistance, unable to even speak, only to see a bunch of dumbfounded looks among the sheep standing by watching the scene unfold. No help there. In seconds, I was going to be a snack on Señor Bath Salts' menu, and I'd end up another fatality in a viral "News of the Weird" story.

I was about to pass out when finally, I snapped. I went into full-on batshit mode and let my survival instincts take over. I reached down and drew the Kahr CW45 that I always carry on my right hip, placing it under the dude's left ear and firing. The bullet exited his skull at an angle that saved me from accidentally shooting an innocent bystander, but brains and blood sprayed out all over the people who were standing on that side of the crowd.

As I rolled the guy's now limp body off me, people scattered everywhere, their screams and shouts erupting all around me. A quick glance around revealed that a few people were still recording the scene on their phones, but from several yards away. I looked over at the guy I'd just been trying to save, saw the exit wound, then promptly turned my head and barfed. It wasn't like I hadn't seen wounds like that before, but I'd nearly been choked to death, I was still having the panic attack from hell, and frankly the idea that I'd just killed the guy wasn't sitting well with me at all.

I could hear people starting to react to what had just happened. More murmurs, some outraged voices, others shouting and arguing. I heard tones of disbelief, angry voices —still others were speaking in dickheadese.

"Did you see what happened? That guy with the scarred up face just killed that poor homeless person!"

"Man, this is going to get, like, a million hits! O-freaking-M-G dude, this is going to blow up my followers!"

"I would have done the exact same thing, absolutely. He did the only thing he could have done. Yep, the only thing."

Again, I tuned them out and my training kicked in as I began assessing myself for injuries and scanning the scene for further threats. I heard sirens, but they weren't from an ambulance pulling up. It was Constable Randy Taylor, the local law dog. I holstered my weapon and stood up with my hands away from my body and in clear sight. Randy got out of his cruiser, weapon drawn, then he saw me and the guy on the ground and quickly holstered it. He reached up to click his radio mike, rattled off something to his dispatcher, and quickly shuffled over to me.

"Randy, it was self-defense. Honest. I was doing CPR on

the guy, and then he just jumped up and started choking the shit out of me. Couldn't get him off me, and I was going out. Had to do it." I had my hands on my knees at this point. I was starting to hyperventilate again.

Randy strode up and grabbed me by the arm, dragging me over to the front of the building, whispering in my ear. "Aidan buddy, I'm going to pretend that what you just said was, 'It was self-defense and I need to speak to my attorney before giving a statement.' Sound good?"

I nodded. He'd just reminded me that anything I said could be used against me in a court of law. For the most part, our county was fairly conservative, and would likely look favorably on a justified self-defense shooting. However, you never knew when you'd get an assistant DA who might be itching to make a name for herself, and that could lead to charges, even if the cops on scene reported that it appeared to be self-defense.

Despite the fact that I have a Mick name, I hardly look like a poster child for the Aryan race. Take one overzealous prosecutor and add an all-white jury who could be convinced that this was just one drunk Mexican killing another drunk Mexican, and I'd be sent up for twenty and change. No thanks. So, I took Randy's cue and zipped it.

Randy sorted of hunkered down in front of me and looked me in the eye. "You know SOP says I have to take you in on a shooting fatality. That means in cuffs. You okay with that?"

I nodded, and allowed him to take my sidearm and cuff me before leading me back to his cruiser. The windows were tinted, the motor and AC were running, and it was cool and quiet inside. I noticed that Randy had left the cuffs loose, and I realized he was actually doing me a favor by putting me in the patrol car.

I sat there for about 30 minutes while Randy and several sheriff's deputies took statements and kept the crowd from tampering with evidence. It took about ten more minutes for an EMS crew to arrive, but they were really only there to transport the body to the morgue. One of them stopped by the patrol car to check me for injuries, but I waved him off and signed an AMA form. Soon after, Randy strolled over and hopped into the front seat of the vehicle.

He remained silent until we'd pulled away from the scene and got down the road a bit. "Witnesses all pretty much said the same thing. You stopped to help the guy, he collapsed, you did CPR, and then he attacked you. We grabbed a couple of cell phones that recorded the events. A couple of folks weren't too happy about it, but they said they wanted to help. Told 'em they can come by the station and get them back after we've copied the videos over."

He paused and looked back over his shoulder. "Looks like it was a justifiable shooting. Not a jury in the county that would put a good Samaritan war hero in jail, no how."

I barked a short laugh, and Randy chuckled in response. "Well, maybe if the DA played it just right. But the thing is, I'm pretty sure I can make this go away before it even gets that far. With the video, we should be able to show that you acted in self-defense. The fact that you were providing aid before the attack will likely clinch it. Case closed."

Randy attempted to make small talk after that, but I just wasn't in the mood. Soon he got the picture and we rode in silence until we pulled up to the Sheriff's office about 20 minutes later. Randy opened the back door and helped me out, and I followed him inside. Despite Randy's assurances, I decided to have a local attorney show up at the station. He sat with me as I gave my statement to the investigator who worked homicide for the county. Three hours after that, I was released without charges filed. Before being released I was told not to leave the area, just in case they needed me for further questioning. The lawyer told me he thought no charges would be filed. I had my doubts, but there was nothing I could do.

One thing was for sure, though; I was still freaking out. It was all I could do to hold things together while I sat through questioning. All the deep breathing exercises and other mental tricks I'd learned weren't working, and I knew the only thing that would cure this and settle me back down was either a shit-load of Xanax, or heading out into the woods to be by myself for a good long while.

I decided to do both, but not necessarily in that order. So after Randy took me to get my truck, I headed straight home to pack my gear for a long trip to the boonies.

[2]
MISSILES

ONE THING I quickly discovered after coming back from Afghanistan was that living in the sticks did a world of good for my head. Maybe it was the Native American in me that I got from my mom's side, but I felt closer to God out in nature than I ever did in church. Mom was Catholic and dad was Protestant, so I spent a lot of time at church growing up. Church didn't stick, but the faith did. Call it superstition, or just wishful thinking, but I'd always felt a deep and abiding Presence in the wilderness that I'd never felt anywhere else. Bottom line was that out in the sticks was the only place I ever really felt at peace. Well, there and hunting terrorists.

I suppose that's why when I first came home, I spent six months living between my family's hunting cabin and several primitive camps I'd set up on our ranch in the Texas Hill Country. The land had been in my family for generations, and included several thousand acres along the Frio River north of Leakey, Texas. It was worth a bundle now, what with all the rich folks from Austin and San Antone wanting to come out here and settle, but my dad was stubborn and refused to sell.

Good on him. Besides, he didn't need the money. Dad had bucked the family tradition of ranching, and instead had gone to school and gotten into insurance. He now owned a thriving insurance agency in a suburb of Austin. This meant I had the ranch and cabin all to myself, and that was how I liked it. My parents respected my need for isolation, so they more or less left me alone out here year round.

Due to the nature therapy more than anything, things had been getting better for me lately. I wasn't experiencing as much social anxiety anymore, so I'd started taking classes at the university extension down in Uvalde. The plan was to apply to physician's assistant school once I had all my prerequisites out of the way. I found out back in Afghanistan that I liked saving people a whole lot better than I liked killing them, and figured it was time to do some good in the world for a change.

But even when my brain was healthy, I liked staying out at the ranch. Any time I spent there was a chance to relive some of the best memories of my childhood. When I was a kid, I'd always looked forward to holidays and summers spent visiting my grandparents out there, and weekends spent hunting with my dad and granddad were always a treat. Everything I knew about hunting and stalking game in these hills I'd learned from my grandpa, and it was knowledge that had served me well in the mountains of Kunar and Nuristan many years later.

But despite all the progress I'd made, my run-in with Señor Bath Salts had definitely triggered an episode. So I headed out to one of my more remote camps just as soon as I got home from the sheriff's office. Sure, the cops had said I needed to stick around, but I interpreted that as meaning "don't leave the county." I called my attorney before I went traipsing off into the boonies and told him that I'd be indisposed for a few weeks. He didn't like it, but agreed to handle things should the cops decide they needed another interview.

Whatever. I'd resigned myself to the fact that what was going to happen would happen, and there was nothing I could do about it. I needed some space and time to clear my head, and that's what I was going to get. I'd built my destination campsite a few months earlier, way the hell out in the middle of nowhere. I set myself up for an extended stay in the primitive A-frame cabin I had at the site.

But no sooner than I'd gotten settled in, it started raining like the first day of Noah's forty. I hunkered down in the cabin for the first week and watched it pour, then finally I got bored and decided to hunt for some fresh meat. After a few hours and a good soaking I got lucky and bagged a couple of rabbits that I found hunkered down in a brush pile. But, as luck would have it, I also caught a monumental case of walking pneumonia.

By the next morning I was delirious with fever and way too weak to hike back to the main house on the ranch. I set out some pots and pans to gather rainwater, then I bundled up on my cot and tried not to die from fever and exposure. Besides the occasional trip to the front door of the cabin to piss and retrieve enough water to prevent my imminent demise, I stayed more or less on my back for the better part of two weeks. Probably the only thing that saved me was a stash of antibiotics that I had in my pack, and some expired ibuprofen that I found in my first aid kit. Well, that and the fact that I'm too damned stubborn to die from my own stupidity.

———

It took me a couple of days after the fever broke to gather enough strength to get up and move around. I soon managed to build a fire and made some broth using the bouillon cubes I always kept in my pack. By the next morning I was back on solid food, and by that evening I was ready to get back to the main cabin for a shower and a good hot meal.

After being out of commission for so long, I decided I'd check in on civilization by tuning into the news on the little emergency weather radio I kept in my pack. It worked on solar power, or I could charge it with a hand crank, and I'd found it to be a handy addition to my typical load out. Besides giving me a way to get weather intel, if I ever got too lonely out in the sticks I could always tune into the nearest country station and get really depressed.

I cranked the handle for about a minute or so and started flipping through the FM stations. All I got was static, so I switched over to the AM dial. It took me a while, but eventually I tuned into a station that broadcast from way out west of us. The signal was weak, but after dialing it in and playing with its antenna, I heard the familiar klaxon that indicated an Emergency Broadcast System test was underway. Annoyed, I turned off the radio and busied myself for a few moments, then I turned it back on, only to hear the same ear-splitting racket. That got me spooked, so I turned it up a notch or two and listened to what followed.

"This is not a test. Repeat, this is not a test. Please listen to the following message in full and follow all instructions carefully. This message will repeat. Again, listen carefully and follow these instructions to ensure the safety of you and those around you."

At that I turned the volume up as a high as it could go. Within seconds the measured cadence of the president's voice came loud and clear from the speakers.

"At 1:26 am on October 3rd, the United States suffered a surprise joint nuclear attack carried out by China, Russia, and North Korea that targeted several large metropolitan areas along the eastern and western seaboards, as well as select cities in the midwestern and southern states. These attacks were apparently carried out with the intention of destroying our largest population areas and infrastructure. Missiles carrying nuclear warheads were detonated in air burst attacks, so as to produce the greatest damage to property and people.

"We are not taking this attack lying down. Already, our military has launched precision nuclear counterstrikes against key targets in China, Russia, and North Korea as well as targets in Iran and Syria. We believe we have prevented further attacks from occurring; however, the damage to our nation's greatest population centers and infrastructure has

been severe. We are doing everything we can to restore communications and power across the mainland, as well as to restore communications with Alaska, Hawaii, and Puerto Rico. We are mobilizing the Army National Guard and FEMA to set up relief camps, field medical facilities, and emergency shelters a safe distance from all areas that have been hit the hardest by these attacks.

"Since the missiles were detonated while airborne, fallout has been minimal in the areas surrounding the attacks. Even so, survivors are encouraged to avoid the blast zones and to escape to the nearest relief center as soon as they are physically capable.

"Unfortunately, the worst effects of these attacks will not be limited to the initial death toll that they have inflicted; it is the panic and chaos caused by these attacks that will likely claim the most lives. Do not panic. Food, water, and shelter will be at a premium in areas that have been hit the hardest, so we ask that you band together with your neighbors and share what resources you have for the good of all until help arrives. Again, we are doing everything we can to provide relief and supplies to the areas that have been affected by these attacks. If you reside in or near one of these areas, please listen to the following message for directions to the nearest emergency relief center for your area. Thank you, and may Allah guide us through this tragedy."

How in the hell did they let a nuclear freaking war happen? I thought to myself as I listened to the long list of relief centers that had been set up since the attacks. I checked my watch and realized that it had been a full three weeks since the missiles hit. Here I was, stuck out in The-Middle-of-Nowhere, Texas, out of my mind with fever while the end of the world as we know it was going down. Who'da thunk it?

As I worked my way mentally through the situation at hand, I made a few assumptions. One, because there were relatively few targets of major military interest in Austin and San Antonio, the damage might not be too severe. Heck, I even hoped for a moment that they might not have been hit at all. But a few minutes later, I heard relief center locations being broadcast for Austin and San Antonio, which blew my hopes clean out of the water. Why anyone would hit those cities out of anything but sheer evil and spite was beyond me. I mean, you truly had to be an evil son of a bitch to bomb millions of people needlessly. Sometimes, I really hated being part of the human race.

Regardless, I figured they'd hit Lackland with a warhead large enough to take out the operations command center there, which would make sense if they were planning to invade the third coast. They'd probably hit Austin for the hell of it, since no major military targets of interest existed in or around the capitol. More than likely Ft. Hood and Ft. Bliss had gotten wiped clean off the map, and Alamogordo was probably toast as well. But if they were aiming for the capitol in Austin and used a smaller nuclear device to take it out, folks five kilometers or so from downtown could have gotten through the blast wave with only minor injuries, which would mostly have been from broken windows and flying debris. So, I was guessing that Mom and Dad were probably fine, but even so they'd need to get the hell out of Dodge fast.

As soon as the social structure started breaking down it'd be chaos, and I didn't want them anywhere near a major metropolitan area once the food riots and pillaging started.

It only took me a half-hour or so to get everything packed and ready, so I sat in the light of the fire I'd stoked up and waited for dawn. As I rested in the near-dark of my campfire, I reflected on how calm I felt. Having a mission and a purpose always seemed to help me keep my shit together back in Afghanistan, and I supposed it should be no different now that I was Stateside. By the time the sun peeked over the hills to the east, I'd already eaten and had a couple of cups of instant coffee in me, and I was good to go. More than good, strangely; I felt fully alive for the first time since coming back home. Chuckling to myself at the irony, I checked the eastern sky for smoke or perhaps the remnants of mushroom clouds, but it was still overcast and I couldn't see a damned thing.

The wind came from the northwest as it had for weeks, which meant that I'd never been in any danger of fallout radiation exposure. Besides, air bursts were the most effective way to destroy a city, and if the emergency broadcast message was accurate, there'd be little to worry about as far as fallout was concerned. However, that also meant that the detonations would have generated a significant EMP blast, which meant all sophisticated electronics would be fried for quite some distance around the blast areas.

That also meant cell phones would be out of service, although some towers that didn't sustain damage might reset automatically. Landlines might work, but it was iffy. Power would definitely be a bust in and near the cities. Some automobiles would be fried, what with the modern computer circuitry that most cars relied on these days. The Internet would be a wash as well, as would most mass communications in general. Thankfully I kept a shortwave radio at the cabin, and had a landline hooked up there, too. Hopefully I'd be able to contact my parents via one method or another, if only to find out if they were okay. I'd certainly be in better shape than most to travel and rescue them, since my Toyota ran on pre-80's tech, and I always kept a spare set of fuses, ignition points, and the like around, along with extra fan belts and other parts I might need in an emergency. So even if it wouldn't start, I was sure I could get it running in short order.

My plan was to head into town, get those supplies that I'd been planning to pick up the day of the shooting, and then drive in a general northeasterly direction along the back roads to get to my folks. Then I'd bring them back out here, and figure out what to do next once I knew they were safe. Dad was smart; he'd know that he needed to either stay put to avoid radiation fallout or get out as quickly as possible. He'd also know how to secure transportation to get him and Mom out of Dodge. I needed to get in touch with them before I took off, just to make sure they'd stay put until I got there.

––––––––

I REACHED the cabin a few hours later. The first thing I did was go out and try to start the Toyota; it started right up with no issues, which somewhat surprised me. EMP was a phenomena that scientists still didn't have a firm grip on, and

I'd read conflicting reports about what could happen after a nuclear attack. Some experts had said the entire grid would go down and all electronics would fail, while others said effects would be localized and civilization could continue.

But even though my truck was working, I wasn't betting on things being copacetic closer into the cities. I had a sneaking suspicion that my truck was working because it was made in the Stone Age—and besides that, you just couldn't kill a Hilux. That was why I'd bought it and restored it. I once saw one buried in a high-rise building demolition on television, and it started right up once they dug it out of the rubble. I had my doubts that more modern auto tech would fare so well.

After ensuring that the truck was working, I went inside and tried to call my parents. I got nothing but a busy signal, even after trying for the better part of half an hour. I started gathering up everything I'd need for a rescue mission to north Austin:

- Extra gas cans. I snagged two five-gallon jerry cans and threw them in the bed of the truck. They were empty, but I could fill them in town. I also snagged an old garden hose to use for siphoning gas from dead cars and trucks along the way.
- Spare parts. I kept spare fuses, points, and so on in the truck. I threw in an extra fan belt for good measure, and beefed up my tool bag with a few extra sockets and wrenches.

- Other tools. I figured a hand winch would be a must for clearing stalled vehicles, so I threw my power puller in the back. I also tossed a Fat Max demo tool and my tactical tomahawk behind the seat. Both might come in handy should I have to do some tactical B&E along the way. I also grabbed some bolt cutters for good measure, as they always came in handy. I already had my Bowie knife on my belt and a tactical folder in my pocket—I never went anywhere without a good knife.

- Weapons. I grabbed my Glock 21, along with my concealment holster. No reason to draw attention on the road. I replaced my Kahr with the Glock, and took the time to switch out the clip on the Kahr so I could wear it on my left side in an appendix carry. The Glock went on my right hip. I grabbed my range bag with two extra mags for the Kahr and four for the Glock, along with two boxes of .45 JHP. I also snagged my M4A1 with six extra mags and a brick of 500 rounds. I kept a red dot sight on it, but could switch to my ACOG if needed, also packed. I brought along a tactical flashlight and a collapsible bipod for the rifle. The bipod added weight, but I liked the stability for long shots.

- Food and shelter. I'd be sheltering in the truck if I had to stop overnight. No way would I leave it to get hot-wired by thieves. I threw my pack in the front seat with all my essentials: sleeping bag, ground mat, portable water filter, water bladder and bottles, iodine tabs, flashlight, and so on. I also threw a 12-pack of bottled water in the floorboard, just for safety's sake. For food, I grabbed some of the dehydrated meals I typically carried into the sticks, along with some summer sausage and jerky. Thankfully, when you have a thousand acres of land to hunt there's no waiting for deer season. I always kept some hard candy in the glove box, along with some high-energy snack bars. I could eat those if the other stuff ran out. I wasn't counting on finding a lot of food along the way, because folks would be clearing the stores out in short order. Those who hadn't prepared were going to be in some deep shit, most assuredly.

- Comms. I had a CB in the truck, but fat lot of good it might do me. I'd snag a cell phone and charger off the first dead person I found. I know, it sounds cruel, but experience had taught me that I'd probably come across more than a few before this was over. Like I said, cell towers might come back online, and it'd be worth it to have the cell if that happened.

Despite being prepared as hell for an event like this, I still wanted to stock up on long-term supplies before I took off. Plus, I needed gas for the truck. I didn't want to hit the supermarket in town due to the crowds. I decided to hit the local Stop N' Steal for gas and whatever else I could get. I had enough cash on me to clear them out of dry goods, and I also planned to get more bottled water and some OTC drugs. It'd have to do.

I loaded what I was going to take with me into the truck, hid it under a tarp inside the camper shell, and drove off to take care of my last-minute chores before I headed out to Austin.

As I PULLED into the gas station, I immediately noticed things were off. For one, there were no cars lined up waiting to get gas. None. If there was any gas to be had, I'd expected to have to wait in line for a while to get it. To pull up and see that there weren't any cars lined up at the pumps made me hella nervous. I wondered if they'd already run out and I was just too late, or maybe the power had gone out and the pumps were out of order.

Could have been any number of things, considering the circumstances. I pulled up to the pumps anyway and went inside to see what was up. A glance at the prices on the sign out front told me that price gouging was in full effect. Twelve bucks a gallon. Ouch. Maybe the prices had scared all the customers off.

As I walked up to the front door, I noticed some fresh blood spatters on the glass. That got my hackles raised right up, so I drew my Glock and kept it hidden behind my leg as I peeked inside the store from behind the corner of the wall. No one was visible, but there was a helluva lot of mess inside the store. I could see more blood splattered all over the floor, as well bloody handprints on the counter. Looked like a robbery, but there were no cops, no alarms, no crime scene tape, and nothing to indicate there were any dead bodies around.

Maybe Randy and the boys from the sheriff's office were busy elsewhere. I could only imagine what was going on in town. People must have been freaking out and raising all kinds of hell. For the most part, the good folks of Leakey were as kind as could be, pretty much overflowing with Texas hospitality and such. But I'd seen what war could do to people, and knew that when ordinary folks were faced with extraordinary circumstances, they'd go to extraordinary lengths to protect and preserve life, limb, and family.

Bottom line, though, was that I still needed gas. The lights were on, so that was a good sign. I could probably still get gas, even if no one was around. I'd leave some cash in the register or drop it in the safe; no need to steal from my neighbors. Not yet, anyway. I cracked the door and propped it open with my foot so I could listen to what was going on inside before entering.

It was quiet as a mouse's house. All I could hear was some water dripping, and the low hum of the walk-in coolers in the back. I listened for a good minute or so, and didn't hear anything else. I opened the door a bit more and called out.

"Hey, anyone in here? I need some gas. I'm not here to rob you. I have money and will pay."

Silence.

I kept my sidearm at low ready and walked in the store. As I stepped inside, I nearly busted my ass by slipping in a pool of blood hidden by the news racks at the front door. I caught my balance by grabbing one of the racks, and looked down to see about two pints of coagulating blood on the floor. Yeah, it was blood alright—no mistaking that smell. I wiped my feet on the entry runner and moved through the store, clearing it one area at a time. I checked behind the counter, then down each aisle using the store mirrors and some good old fashioned door kicker moves. Then finally I cleared the office, the rest rooms, storage area, and the walk-ins.

The place was a mess, and emptier than a synagogue on Superbowl Sunday. There were more random blood stains and spatters, and someone had tracked blood all over the store as well. Scratch that, make that two—no, three some-ones. Two of them didn't look like they were doing so hot. One of them looked like he was limping, and another was shuffling with a strange gait. Reminded me of someone doing opium. Saw enough of that in Afghanistan to know what it looked like.

One thing was obvious: they were both chasing the third person. Looked to be a female; shoes were small, with no tread and a narrow toe. Tracks led out the back door, and I saw more bloody handprints on the door release bar. I listened at the door, but heard nothing. I swung it open and looked left and right. Nothing but a retention wall and some trash.

This was all really messed up, and I was pretty damn

curious what had happened to these people. But, first things first. I went behind the counter and turned on the pump I needed, then popped open the cash register and left a few twenties in there. I went to shut the drawer, and then thought better of it and left another twenty. Damned if I was going to pay twelve bucks a gallon, though. Then I went out to the truck and left the pump running while I started loading up.

I snagged three cases of bottled water, which was all they had left. I also scored two boxes of Power Bars and all their jerky. I took every bit of toilet paper they had, along with some jumper cables, a few quarts of oil, a roll of duct tape, some radiator repair tape, a bottle of Gorilla glue, and all their OTC drugs. And a twelve pack of tall boys, just in case I never got to enjoy a cold one again.

I used a hand truck I found in the back and loaded it all up. I gave the place one final look around and found a first aid kit in the office, so I cleaned that out too. Once I got it all in the truck, I went back inside to leave them the rest of the cash I had on hand, along with an IOU and a list of what I took in exchange for the rest. I figured I'd shorted them about a hundred bucks, but to hell with it. Better that it was taken by someone who was good for it than by looters.

As I walked back out to the truck to top off the tank and fill my jerry cans, that whole bloody scene inside kept nagging at me. I thought on it a bit and decided it wouldn't take too much time to see where those folks had gone. I threw the gas cans in back, hopped in my truck, and pulled it around back. I flipped it around and backed it into the tree line behind the store, locked it, and picked up the trail at the back door. It headed out back down an old deer trail. I followed it with my sidearm drawn and my eyes peeled.

———

THE DEER TRAIL was fairly unused, so it made for tight quarters as I followed the obvious tracks the three people from the gas station had left. It looked like the girl had made better time than the two shufflers. Her tracks were longer and she was striking hard on her heels with every step. Her trail went on for about a quarter-mile along the trail, then she had cut off at an angle into the trees, presumably to lose her pursuers. I could see that both pursuers had continued down the deer trail a ways, then they had stopped abruptly and shuffled around. After that, their trail went off into the sticks in the same direction as the girl's. I decided to follow the girl's trail. She was moving at speed that had left a clear line of broken branches and scuffed ground to follow.

About a half-mile further, I noticed that the girl had stopped and attempted to hide in some brush. She had hunkered down behind some cedar trees, and it looked like she had crouched there for a while. There were several branches of the tree that had been stripped of foliage, which I presumed she did out of nervousness while waiting to see if she had evaded her pursuers. Unfortunately, she hadn't, as their trail had converged with hers about fifteen yards before. I found what I assumed to be her phone in the brush a few yards out; it was cracked, but otherwise still in working order. I pocketed it and continued to track her.

After that, the trail led out into a short clearing, beyond which was a steep drop-off of about 75 feet that went into a canyon. There appeared to have been a scuffle, and at least one person had gone off the edge into the canyon. I searched carefully for some sign that the girl had escaped, but unfortunately I could find no further sign of her passing. I walked up to the edge of the drop-off and looked down, and saw three bodies tangled up in the brush at the bottom. It was hard to see clearly exactly what I was looking at, but I doubted anyone could have survived that fall.

I shook my head and said a silent prayer, then went to head back to the gas station. Just as I was turning away, I thought I saw movement from the bottom of the canyon out of the corner of my eye. I looked quickly back, but didn't detect anything else from the corpses below. I chalked it up to the wind, coyotes, or just my mind playing tricks on me. I made a mental note to tell Randy just as soon as I ran across him, and headed back to my truck.

———

ONCE I GOT to my truck, I sat for a moment and tried to process what I'd seen. A lot of it didn't make sense. For one, where did all the blood come from? I had found some blood on the trail, but based on what I'd seen in the store, whoever had lost all that liquid would've been in no shape for a hike in the woods. And why the heck were those two guys chasing that girl? The beer cooler was mostly left untouched, the cash register was full, and I couldn't for the life of me figure out why they left the cash and took off after her. Could've been to rape her, sure. But every crook I'd ever known would get the cash first, then they'd go after other objectives. Even criminals have their priorities.

Also, there were no signs of gunfire inside the store. There had been a struggle, but I hadn't found any loose casings or bullet holes anywhere. I supposed they could have taken their time to pick them up, but I doubted those two shufflers would've bothered. From what I could tell, they both had been so strung out I doubted either had been thinking coherently. That being said, they had still been with it enough to chase a girl through the woods to her death. How all three ended up going over was anyone's guess.

I decided to consider it an unsolved mystery and leave it for Dennis Farina to figure out. As tragic as it all was, I had more important things to think about. Namely, getting to Austin intact and rescuing my aging parents from God-knew-what was going to happen once the shit hit the fan. I figured the first thing that would happen would be the looting, followed by food riots, then roving gangs. The good news was that Mom and Dad lived in a nicer area of town, far away from where most of the criminal element lived. The bad news was that they lived exactly where I would go to find victims were I an enterprising criminal facing a nuclear apocalypse.

Not cool. I decided to pull out the girl's cell phone and try to give Mom a call. I got a low battery indicator, so I headed back into the store to snag a cell charger. I drove back to the cabin the long way, just to see what was going on elsewhere in this one horse town. I cruised on down toward Leakey, telling myself that I was just going to look around and avoid contact with anyone. Just for insurance, I slapped a magazine in my rifle and put it barrel down in the passenger footwell, out of sight, where I could grab it if I needed.

As I drove slowly down the road, I came across a lot of abandoned cars. All were newer models that relied on fancy computer equipment to keep them running. A car is a sort of Faraday cage, but any exposed antenna will suck in a strong EMP signal like a Dyson in a dust storm. I suspected all those new cars were basically bricked by the EMP generated by the bombs that were dropped on San Antonio and Austin.

I was moving slow enough to avoid colliding with any sudden obstacles that might pop up, but not so fast that I couldn't see inside the cars. All of them were empty, but a few showed signs of violence. Smashed windows, along with plenty of blood and gore. I said another silent prayer, both for those folks and for myself, and wondered if the whole world had gone mad already. I glanced at a few houses as I passed by and saw one or two curtains flutter, but witnessed absolutely no sign of anyone out and about. Obviously, people were scared and hunkering down, and I couldn't blame them after what I had seen.

About a mile out of Leakey I came across a semi-truck pulled off the side of the road. The door was closed, but I could see someone slumped in the cab. I pulled over, grabbed the rifle and the first aid kit I'd snagged at the gas station, and walked over to see if I could help. As I walked up, I could see someone had smeared blood and what I assumed were guts all over the outside of the cab. It also looked like they'd been trying to get inside the cab, banging on the glass and whatnot.

I looked around but saw no sign of anyone nearby. I climbed up on the sideboard and peered inside. Blood and brains had splattered all over the roof of the cab, and the guy had a small hole in his temple. Suicide. I tried the door handle, but it was locked, so I used the glass tool on my folder to break the window, then I opened the door to get the gun. It was a small .38 caliber revolver, cheap but reliable. .38 was a common round, so I took it along with the box of shells the driver had left on the seat. I said another prayer for the old timer, and silently thanked him for the gun and shells. He had a picture of some kids and what I assumed were their parents on his dash; I took it and placed it in his hand, and shut the door.

As I climbed down off the cab, I saw some people approaching from Leakey. Not just some. A whole mob. They were far enough away to give me plenty of time to get in my truck and head back the way I came before they could even get close enough to be a threat. I decided to give up on seeing what things looked like in town. If the looting had already started in the little city of Leakey, Texas, population 425, I needed to get my parents out of Round Rock as soon as possible. I left the mob in my rearview and headed back to the cabin as fast as all the broken down cars and debris on the road would allow.

[4]
UNREAL

ONCE BACK AT the cabin I plugged the girl's cell phone into the charger and tried the landline again. No dice. I left the cell phone on, though, just in case someone tried to reach the girl. I figured I could tell them what had happened and at least give them closure, even though it might make me a suspect in her murder. Considering the circumstances, I thought it was unlikely that the courts would be back in operation anytime soon, but eventually things would return to some level of normalcy, so I decided to turn off the phone after all. No sense getting involved until I spoke with Randy about it.

I felt pretty hungry. The day's events had ended up being a lot more stressful than I had expected. Not that being in a nuclear apocalypse was supposed to be a day at the beach, but I hadn't expected things to be this chaotic and violent so soon. I put some soup on the stove and munched out on some deer sausage and crackers while I waited for the soup to heat, then I tried calling my parents again using the landline. I got nothing but a busy signal, so I decided to keep trying on the odd chance I might get through. Once the cell phone I'd found was charged enough, I'd also start trying to call them on that. Couldn't hurt to try.

Once my soup was ready, I hunkered down in front of the short wave and started scanning the freqs for some news of what was going on out there in the big wide world. Nobody seemed to know exactly what had happened, but we did know who fired the first shot. Apparently the North Koreans decided to drop the bomb on Seoul, and that started a whole chain of events that had ended with the U.S., Russia, and China tossing nuclear weapons at each other. It would have been only a matter of time before something like this happened. I mean, once you let the crazies build nukes, the logical conclusion is that eventually they're going to use them. Heck, even a ten-year-old could see that.

Thankfully, something major happened that caused the powers that be to stop just short of total global annihilation. Apparently some greater threat had appeared out of the blue, but due to conflicting reports I couldn't get a clear picture of just what that was exactly. Some said it was a global pandemic, others said aliens, while still others were yammering about an impending zombie apocalypse. Go figure. I was more likely to believe the alien invasion scenario than I was the zombie thing. Come on, zombies? I love Romero films as much as the next guy, but that was just a little too far out there for me to believe.

Still, there were some pretty hairy reports about massive

riots and waves of civil unrest hitting large cities all across the globe. There was also some talk about cannibalism, which wasn't surprising if you took into account just how close to starvation much of the global population was at any given moment. Throw in a little hysteria and confusion, and it was easy to see that most of this stuff was hearsay being blown out of proportion. Even so, it made me worry that much more for my folks.

Strangely, reports were coming in of violence even in countries where no nuclear attacks had occurred. Even small nations across the African continent, and island nations and territories like Haiti and Puerto Rico reported they were also experiencing massive waves of violence, rioting, and looting. Again, I figured this was just human nature rearing its ugly head. Most folks with half a brain who hadn't prepared for something like this would figure out pretty quick that they needed to secure the essentials if they wanted to survive. Add in the fact that roughly 1 in 25 people showed sociopathic tendencies in modern society, and you had the makings for some serious fan-hitting shit.

My only consolation was that my dad was a self-reliant son of a bitch. He had been assigned to Force Recon in the Corps, and had seen some pretty hairy shit while he was active. Understandably he never spoke about it much, but the old man was tough as nails, and I believed he could turn into a stone killer if need be. He'd also do anything to keep my mom safe, and kept an arsenal of firearms in their house along with enough ammo to keep a small army at bay. He'd likely dig in for a while until he knew it was safe, then he'd secure reliable transport and bug out as soon as he was able. I just hoped I'd be able to speak to them before he decided it was time to beat feet.

After finishing my meal and listening to the shortwave for about an hour, I decided to check my battery bank and the solar panels I'd put in earlier in the year. I had installed eight panels on the roof where it got the most southern exposure, along with a bank of batteries in an attached shed that sat alongside the cabin. Since the system was tied to the grid, I'd also set it up so I could disconnect the house from the power company and run off my battery bank and panels. Being a natural worry wart, I grabbed a flashlight and headed outside to check the condition of the batteries. I'd gone with sealed gel cells both for the cost and for the lack of maintenance, but I figured it couldn't hurt to make sure none were showing signs of failure. Once I was sure the system was in good working order, I locked it up and headed back inside for the night.

After that, there was really nothing I could do but keep trying to call my folks and hope for the best. Dad's vehicles were probably knocked out by the EMP, so he'd need to secure transport before heading out. That could take him while, depending on how bad things got, which meant he might just decide to bunker in place. I really wanted to get a lock on my parent's location before I left, but finally decided that if I didn't get them on the phone by morning, I'd head for Austin and hope I got to them before Dad decided to blow town. I continued listening in on the shortwave and calling every 15 to 20 minutes, until I finally dozed off on the couch sometime after midnight.

———

THE SOUND of creaking floorboards on my front porch woke me up at about zero-three-thirty, according to my watch. I still had my Glock on me and my M4 was leaning up against the side table close at hand. I slipped on my boots, listening for any additional noise from outside. While it could have easily been an animal, no raccoon was going to be loud enough to make those boards creak. Only thing that heavy would be a black bear, which I'd only seen once in all my years on the ranch. That, or a human. I was betting on the latter, although how someone would have found our place at random was a mystery to me. This cabin was well back up in the woods from the main road, and it'd take an aerial search team and a FLIR camera to find it in the dark.

No matter. I assumed it was someone who'd headed out in the woods to bug out and stumbled across the place. Or possibly an illegal—I found them on the ranch all the time. If it was a looter I'd try to scare them off, and if it was an illegal, I'd just give them some food and send them on their way.

As I was reaching for my rifle, in my grogginess I accidentally caused my soup bowl to collide with the table lamp. Although the sound wasn't really that loud, it may as well have been a gunshot in the silence of the Hill Country night.

Immediately after that, I could hear a pair of heavy feet shuffling to the door, followed by scraping and banging on the frame and door itself.

Must be a drunk, I thought to myself. But that in and of itself was a pretty damned deep mystery. How in the hell would a drunk make it up a mile of dirt roads and jeep trails in the middle of the night? Let me tell you, it gets pitch dark up here after sundown, and on an overcast night like this one you're lucky to see two feet in front of your face without a flashlight or some other artificial light source. If whoever it was had come in a vehicle, then I'd have heard them coming up the road. As far as I could tell there weren't any flashlights swinging around outside, either.

I figured it was time to take a look, so I crept over to the window and peeked out. All I could see was a large, dark figure swaying back and forth, more or less bumping into and banging on the door and wall outside. Deciding that this was just a little too weird, even for my tastes, I crept over to my gun safe and popped it open. I used just a sliver of light from my mini taclight to see the dial so I could crack it open, and grabbed my NVGs from inside. Strapping them onto my head, I turned them on with my eyes closed and cranked down the brightness, then opened my eyes and waited for them to adjust. After about 30 seconds or so, I headed to the second bedroom.

When I was about 14, I'd made an emergency egress point, otherwise known as a trap door, in my bedroom floor here at the cabin. Originally, I'd made it so I could sneak out and go frogging and coon hunting in the middle of the night, although when my dad found out he threw a fit. My grandpa calmed him down, saying he'd always wanted to do the same thing when he was a kid. Since Grandpa overruled Dad on all things having to do with the cabin and land, I got to keep my trap door. These days I kept the hinges well-oiled and the latch maintained, just in case I ever needed a way to get out of the cabin without making a lot of noise. This would be one of those times.

Secretly praying that no rattlesnakes had taken up residence under the house recently, I carefully lowered my rifle down the hole and on the ground below, and crawled out head first. It was a tight fit, and I recalled how much easier this had been as a kid. After getting my bearings, I tucked my rifle over my arm to keep it from scraping the ground, and began to low crawl out from under the house. I could still hear my guest banging and scratching at the front door the whole time, which pretty much covered any noise I made. Once I was out from under the cabin, I press-checked my rifle to make sure I had a round chambered, and headed around the house.

Coming around the corner, I could get a much better look at the guy through my NVGs. At first glance, he looked like he was either extremely muddy, or that he'd been in an accident and was covered in blood. A head injury could account for his strange behavior, so I assumed the latter. It looked like he had suffered a nasty cut over his eye; there was blood all over his face. As I crouched and watched him from around the corner of the cabin, something niggled at the back of my mind. His movements and behavior were strangely familiar, but I just couldn't place them.

Then it clicked. The way this guy was moving reminded me a lot of the illegal who'd attacked me at the Stop N' Steal. That guy had moved with the same rhythmic swaying motion, and with the same repetitive pattern as well. Weird. I decided to sit tight and observe him for a moment, since he didn't appear to be an immediate threat. I leaned against the cabin and made myself more comfortable so I could keep an eye on him for a few minutes.

Strangely, the guy's pattern of movement never changed. He just kept sort of banging on and walking into the door, over and over again. To be honest, after a while watching him started to put me to sleep, so I'd look away every now and again and scan the area for other threats. With nothing changing after about ten minutes or so, I was about to call it a night and go back inside.

Then there was a loud rustling from the treeline behind me. Likely it was a rabbit or a squirrel evading a night predator, but it sounded like thunder in the still silence of the night. I turned to look, just in case it was another human instead of an animal, but couldn't see anything. When I turned back to see if my guest had noticed, I got the shock of my life.

My visitor had turned fully toward me to see what had made all the racket, and now that he did I could see that this gentleman wasn't well. For starters, he was missing half the right side of his face, which looked like it had either been torn or gnawed off. He was similarly missing his right arm at the elbow, which ended in a nasty, jagged wound that should have been dripping blood all over. It was instead dry and crusty, like a newly scabbed cut.

Finally, the guy's throat had been ripped out.

His throat had been ripped the hell out. And he was still moving around. *Shit.*

The impact of what I was seeing though my NVGs freaked me out so bad that I stumbled. And as I reached out to the wall to steady myself, I missed it completely and fell to one knee, making a shitload of noise as I bumped into the cabin wall. That sure got his attention. Before I could get back to my feet, he was moaning up a storm and making a beeline for me, despite it being blacker than charcoal on a cast iron kettle out here.

I got my bearings and started backing up, mumbling to myself, "This isn't happening, this is not happening, holy shit, this is really happening!" Well, maybe I screamed that last part like a little girl, because Stumpy the one-armed freak was gaining on me as I was backing up. I yelled at him, as loud as I could, "Stop, or I will be forced to shoot!" That only seemed to make him even more agitated, and the sum' bitch picked up his pace.

I knew that I couldn't keep backing up or I was going to go ass over teakettle on a branch or rock and have this asshole right on top of me. Once I came to that conclusion, it was abundantly clear what I had to do.

"Screw this," I declared, and fired two rounds center mass on the guy.

No effect.

"Ah, shit!" I switched the selector from select fire to full auto and lit the guy up. I emptied a mag in him, which made him jerk about like a puppet and seemed to halt his progress as he staggered about. Unfortunately, once I ran out of ammo, he kept coming.

"Balls!" I shouted out as I reached for another magazine and realized I'd come outside without a spare. I dropped the M4 on my one-point harness and drew my Glock.

The guy was within a few paces of me when I drew a bead on his big ugly forehead. Up close I could see he was some type of office worker. He wore a short-sleeved oxford and a tie, both covered in gore that went all the way down to his cheap Walmart khakis. His knees were also covered in blood, which I assumed meant he'd been kneeling in it. He was missing one brown dress shoe, and I could see that he'd worn through a sock and most of the flesh on that foot. His other shoe, strangely, was polished to a high gloss, and besides some scuff marks on the toe, was more or less free of blood.

Weird, the things you notice when you think you're about to die. I took all this in within a millisecond, and pulled the trigger twice. The first round made a nice neat hole in his forehead and snapped his head back, and the second one caught him in what would have been his windpipe. The freak fell at my feet immediately, dead as—well, a corpse. I shuffled back a bit anyway and kept my muzzle trained on him for a few seconds, listening to the sound of my heart beating out of my chest and the rapid rhythm of my impending hyperventilation.

I made a conscious effort to slow down my breathing so I didn't pass out. Once the lightheadedness cleared, I shuffled forward in a shooting stance and nudged Stumpy with my toe. No response. I did it a few more times, then I set to kicking the shit out of him with my steel-toed combat boots while spewing a string of obscenities that would make a drunken sailor blush.

Once I'd gotten that out of my system, I bent over and vomited. I must have stayed there, hands on my knees and catching my breath, for—oh, maybe five minutes or so. Once or twice, I heaved again, noticing just how much this guy stank. He reeked of dead flesh. It was a smell I was intimately familiar with, and one I'd hoped to never experience again.

When I'd got back from Afghanistan, I'd applied for a job with the Travis County Coroner's office. After my interview, they took me on a tour of their autopsy room. It was the dead of summer, and they'd run out of space in their meat locker. Yeah, you think you could deal with that smell, but you'd be wrong. Needless to say, I didn't get the job.

All quaint memories aside, I needed to regroup and rethink my plan. Thing was, if the reports I'd been hearing over the shortwave were correct and there really was some sort of zombie outbreak going down, I really couldn't afford to waste time getting to Mom and Dad. Hell, this is bad. Really bad, I thought.

On that note, I crawled back under the house, locked that hatch up tight, double-checked that all the doors and windows were locked, and started slamming that six-pack of tall boys I'd snagged earlier from the gas station. After the fifth one, my nerves had settled and I was finally able to get back to sleep and catch a few more winks to prep for what was to come.

[5]
ENGAGEMENT

I WOKE up a few hours later, still a bit drunk and already feeling a minor hangover coming on. I sat up quickly, remembering the events of the night before. Despite the pounding in my skull, I got up and hopped over to the window. Yep, he was still there, clearly missing a limb, and clearly dead twice over.

"Piss," I hissed quietly. I skulked over to the kitchen, slugged a glass of water and put a kettle on for coffee. Then, I went to the bathroom and carried out my morning routine, finding a clean change of clothes and taking the time to groom myself just like any other day. The routine was to help keep me sane, to keep my spirits up. I had a feeling I was going to need both before the week was over.

About the time that my kettle was whistling at me, the phone rang. I ran into the kitchen to pick it up, pulling the kettle off the stove at the same time. "Hello?"

"Aidan, Aidan is that you?" It was my mom, thank God. I could hear her chattering in the background to my dad, telling him it was me on the line. I heard his deep voice rumbling back, instructing my mother to tell me they were fine.

"Mom, tell Dad I heard him, and that I said to stay put until I get there."

"Oh, *mijo*, everything is okay. Your dad has everything under control, and we're safe as can be here outside of the city. He says to tell you—"

Click. The line went dead. "Mom? Mom, hello?" I hit the receiver and tried to call back. All I got was the same busy signal I'd been getting for the last day or so.

"Damn it to hell!" I shouted, and nearly threw the phone across the kitchen. Instead, I took a few deep breaths and set it down in the cradle. Probably wouldn't have hurt it, as that old bakelite phone had been through hell and back over the years, but I didn't want to risk breaking my comms.

I leaned back against the counter and looked at my options. Option A: Wait to hear from my parents again and make sure they stayed put. Problem with that was there was no way of knowing when or if we'd be able to get through again. So, onto Option B, which was to sit tight and wait for my dad to load up whatever wheels he could find and get here. He would find a means of transport, that was for sure. So no dice. Him and my mom alone on the road, all the way from Austin to here? Uh-uh, no way, no how.

That left Option C. Pack my shit and get my ass in gear.

Action over reaction. Now, there was an option I could live with. I made my coffee and fried some eggs, heating some toast up on the burners and making some bacon as well. Once I'd fueled up and tossed back some aspirin for good measure, I loaded everything I needed into the Toyota and did a once-over around the place to make sure everything was locked down. First order of business was switching the solar system over to start charging the battery bank. No telling how long I'd be gone, and by the time I got back the power might be out for good, so I figured I may as well prepare for that contingency.

It also meant putting the bear shutters on the cabin. My dad had decided to get them a few years back after black bear sightings started increasing in the Hill Country. Glad he did, because they'd do double-duty for fending off these—what, zombies? Living dead? I thought back to that guy I'd put down the night before, and how after I'd punched his ticket he was deader than dead.

"Deaders," I said to myself. That was as good a term as any, and it didn't freak me out quite so bad to think it or say it. Well, at least that was settled.

As for all my valuables, the gun safe would take a forklift to move and a blowtorch to cut through. No way anyone was getting what I had locked up in there. As far as the rest of my weapons and ammo—my real stock of SHTF stuff—that was all buried in caches all around the property and at my camps out in the sticks. Hell if I was going to be caught flat-footed during TEOTWAWKI. Screw that.

I looked around the cabin and supposed I was ready as ever. Then I remembered Stumpy. He was sure to draw animals and Lord knew what else to the cabin. I definitely needed to dispose of him before I left. I wrapped him in an old plastic sheet, taped him up with duct tape, and laid him across the lowered tailgate of my truck, after securing my gear with cargo netting. I'd drop him in a ravine right off the road on my way out of town.

I drove down the old cabin road and hit 336, stopping to lock the gate on the way out. I was about to drive off when I thought better of leaving it exposed. I cut some brush to hide the gate and that shiny brass and steel lock. It wasn't perfect, but it'd do for a short time. Then I got in the truck and boogied off down the road, heading south for Highway 83.

———

ABOUT A MILE down the road I started running into trouble. Never mind the cars that had slowed me down on my first little excursion this way; I'd forgotten about that mob of "looters" that I'd seen coming up the road the day previous. Yeah, those looters turned out to be what looked like the entire population of Leakey, all milling up and down the road looking for somebody's face to chomp on.

They were all deaders. All of them.

I figured out what they ate by observing several packs of them huddled around corpses like a school of piranha, tearing off bits of flesh and skin and fat with their teeth and hands.

Those groups barely paid me any mind as I drove as fast as I could past them. However, if I slowed down too much I drew the swift attention of all those who did not have their own human snack pack to feed on. This resulted in my truck getting beaten on in a few instances, not to mention all the gore they left on the windows. *Nasty.*

Before I even got to Leakey I could see that this wasn't going to work. There were simply too many cars blocking the road, and too many deaders milling about to get through. I briefly considered just running them down, then I came to my senses and remembered what had happened to my dad's full-size Ford truck when he hit a deer doing forty. I doubted that my little truck could take that much abuse, no matter how tough it was.

Moreover, I hated to think about what might happen if I got stuck on a pile of bodies. This truck had a lift kit and four-wheel drive, but I recalled a story a cop had once told me about a woman he arrested for murder. She had tried to run over another girl she had caught with her boyfriend *in flagrante.* The girl had gotten stuck under the car as she ran her over, and she'd dragged that girl three blocks before getting stuck on a curb. I could easily imagine getting two or three of these things stuck in my wheel well, and pictured what that might do to my axles and suspension. No thanks.

As soon as I got the space I hooked around and headed back north for Highway 41. I figured that away from town there'd be almost no cars blocking the roads, and a helluva lot less deaders. Nothing but ranches and hills out that way, so the chances that I'd run into a herd like this one were minimal at best.

Sure enough, I made good time all the way up to 41, and then it was more or less smooth sailing for the next eight or ten miles, up until 41 intersected with 83. Unfortunately, at 83 there was a four car pile-up with a small herd of deaders milling around and beating on an overturned minivan. I suspected that there were some survivors inside the vehicle, so I parked back up the road a few hundred meters and climbed on top of the camper with my rifle and a pair of binos.

I couldn't see much inside the car, but I got busy straight away and started dropping corpses like Ash Williams on speed. Once I'd dropped all the deaders that were milling about the van, I hopped back inside the truck and pulled up close to the crash, leaving me some space to get out quick in case I needed to boogie. None of the corpses were moving, so I decided to jump out and see if there was anyone left alive inside.

As I crept closer to the van, I could see a couple of corpses sitting inside the vehicle. Both people, who I assumed to be husband and wife, were clearly dead. I snuck around the side to see what was causing the deaders to make all that fuss, and saw a tuft of white and brindle moving behind the window. Crouched down in the back amidst a pile of bags, suitcases, golf clubs, and other assorted crap was a large American Bulldog, shivering its ass off.

Lots of people don't know that animals shiver like that to burn off adrenaline, and not necessarily because they're cold or scared. So when your dog freaks out and they start to shiver, it's because nature is telling them to burn that shit off before they screw their brains up. We as humans have lost that capability, therefore we routinely experience shit like nervous breakdowns and panic attacks. Nature got it right the first time, though. There was a guy on the base where I was stationed who worked with soldiers who had PTSD. He taught them a form of exercise that would cause your body to shiver and shake just like that dog was, and guys I knew who did it swore by it. Crazy.

Anyway, I wasn't going to leave this dog here to starve. I went back to the truck, got some jerky and a bottle of water, and worked the back hatch on the van open. That freaked the dog out more, and it started shivering even worse. I knelt down by the hatch and started whispering to it, trying to soothe it and calm it down. Once it settled down a bit, I popped the top on the water and poured some out on the headliner of the vehicle. The dog gladly lapped it up. I poured out more and kept pouring until it was all gone.

I reached in and let it sniff me. Once I got a sniff and a lick, I gave it the jerky. After that, it was just a matter of a few more minutes to coax it out. Once the dog got out of the van, I could see that she was a beautiful example of the Scott standard. Long and lean, but muscular and athletic, these dogs could leap a six foot chain link fence, play chicken with a 1,200 pound bull, and run a mountain lion up a tree, all in a day's work. Damned good dogs.

I just didn't know if I had the ability to keep a dog and myself alive. Still, I couldn't just leave her here, not with the way she was giving me puppy eyes and rubbing up against me. So, I led her over to the truck and let her jump up in the cab. She leaned over and gave me a big, sloppy kiss, and then plopped down on the seat with her chin on her paws, as if to say, "Alright, let's get the hell out of here."

I chuckled and dug out some more jerky for her, and we got the hell out of there.

[6]
FANTASY

I KEPT HEADING up 41 until I got just a few miles short of I-10. I figured I-10 would be a cluster hump, so I'd already planned to head south at Mountain Home and take 27 down to Kerrville. I hated the thought of going through a town the size of Kerrville, since I preferred to stay away from larger population areas after seeing what happened in Leakey, but I didn't really have any choice. I turned south at Mountain Home and headed on down to take my chances with the local residents of Kerrville.

As I headed down 27 south, I meditated on everything that had happened recently and everything that I'd seen. My experiences in the military and in Afghanistan had taught me to compartmentalize my emotions, so I'd been stuffing down a lot of what I felt about the events of the last few days. But while "focus on the mission" was definitely going to be my mantra over the next 48 hours, I still felt compelled to wonder about things that might affect my ability to complete it.

Like, for example, what the hell was causing dead people to walk around and try to eat other people? Was it a bioweapon of some sort? Or a mutated pathogen, maybe something that was altered by the radiation from the bombs? Right now, those two scenarios were the only ideas that made any sense. I briefly entertained the idea that it might be an alien intervention or something supernatural, but I dismissed those scenarios as preposterous, deciding to apply Occam's razor in this instance and call it a pathogen, no matter the source.

But pathogens only affected the living, and thus far all I'd seen were reanimated dead. Sure, you could catch a disease from a dead animal or human, that was a given. But to my knowledge, there wasn't a single organism that could cause a corpse to rise up and start moving around again. The only thing I could think of that might even be remotely able to do something like that were prions, proteins responsible for causing mad cow disease and Creutzfeldt–Jakob disease in humans. Nasty stuff, but prions caused rapid brain tissue degeneration that altered personality and behavior. I really didn't see how they could reanimate a dead person, not within the boundaries of my limited medical knowledge, anyway.

I considered all this as I rolled down the road at about 20 to 25 miles an hour, driving around cars and dodging the odd deader. I hadn't seen many out this way, and I considered stopping and taking them out as I came across them to help stop the spread of whatever infection was causing this, but I realized fairly quickly that this was a lost cause. If most of a town of 400 people could succumb to the disease overnight, then it was going to spread rapidly throughout the population, regardless of whether or not I plugged a few extra deaders for practice. So, I kept on truckin' and didn't even bother to wave as I drove by.

Once I hit a patch of road that was clear of cars and deaders in all directions, I stopped and pulled out my road atlas. According to the sign I'd just passed I was just outside of Ingram, a town of about 1,700 people. That could be tricky. Not as tricky as Kerrville, but tricky. I decided that, so long as there weren't any herds of these things running around, I'd try to stop to refuel while I was there. The truck got decent gas mileage, but I'd already burned half a tank with all the extra driving and near-idling I was doing driving around abandoned cars, wrecks, and ambulatory corpses. So if I could risk it, I would. If not, I'd just hit an abandoned car somewhere after Kerrville and use the siphon I'd snagged from the gas station.

———

AFTER I HAD MY BEARINGS, I shifted back into gear and drove on. But about a half-mile further up the road I saw something that frankly seemed a bit incongruous, considering all the death and mayhem. It was a family of four, sitting on top of an older Suburu SUV, eating sandwiches and drinking sodas. As I pulled over the hill, I could see mom pull her kids closer, while dad started waving and shouting. Obviously, this guy hadn't watched any post-apocalyptic movies, ever. If he had, he'd have those kids and his wife hid off in the woods somewhere while he figured out another means of transport.

A part of me thought back to my wartime days, and I started scanning the trees on either side of the road for an ambush. I stopped the truck and pulled out my binos, and did a good 360 check for any hint that I was being played. I also checked the roadside for possible IEDs. Couldn't be too careful; this was an apocalypse, after all. I didn't really see anything that raised my hackles, so I focused in on the family instead.

Dad was clearly the academic type. He was bespectacled and wearing corduroys, a sweat-stained oxford shirt partially tucked in, tennis shoes, and a bow tie. Mom looked like my third grade teacher. Mousy, docile, and with that mom vibe that all decent men respond favorably to, regardless of age. And the kids were straight out of a Disney movie, just a couple of towheaded, freckled, bright-eyed siblings out for an adventure with their parents.

God help them, but they were in for a shocker. Inwardly, I sighed. *Time to play the good Samaritan.* I drew my Glock and placed it under my thigh as I pulled up alongside them. I left a good ten foot gap between us and rolled down the window, keeping my other hand on the weapon.

"You folks having car trouble?" I asked politely, knowing the answer already. Even so, I knew calm banter would settle them down, and didn't mind saying something idiotic if it meant that they'd feel a little easier about my presence.

The dad nodded. "We ran out of gas. Can you believe it? I left the outskirts of San Antonio with a full tank, but with all the traffic and abandoned cars along the way, we ended up on empty long before I thought we would."

I looked at the wife, who eyed me while she hushed the kids, one of whom was currently pulling the hair of the other. She appeared to be nervous, and was obviously the common sense player in the marriage. I looked back to the dad. "If you don't mind me asking, why didn't you fill up in Ingram?"

He looked at me like I was stupid, which was kind of funny since he was the one sitting there on top of a car with no gas. "Well, I tried, but all the stations were closed, and no one would help us. I thought we might find one outside of town, but we ran out of fuel before I got us very far."

I nodded and pursed my lips. "Might have been better to hunker down in Ingram."

He shook his head. "Oh no, we're on our way to Sarah's parents out near Rock Springs. They have some land out there, and it seemed like the safest bet—I mean, considering what's happened." His wife whispered in his ear, and he whispered something back. Then he climbed down off the roof of the car and jogged over.

He leaned in and spoke softly to me through the window, which momentarily caused me to tighten my hand on the Glock. "Look, mister, I know it's a lot to ask, but I really need your help. Sarah and I have been trying to put a good face on for the kids, but we've been lucky so far. Last night we slept in the car, and one of those things walked by. Thankfully, the kids were asleep, but it's only a matter of time before more come along. You've gotta help me get my family out of here before something happens. All I need is some gas, and we'll be on our way."

He was gripping my arm through the window, and I could see the desperation in his eyes. It was real. He might have been ill-prepared for this event, but he was no fool, and he was just a father trying to save his family. I glanced over at the dog, but she merely gave the guy a sideways glance from one eye, chuffed once, and continued snoozing. I guess he was legit. My mind had already been made up when I'd seen the kids, but this cinched it for me.

I gently peeled his hand off my arm and patted his hand as I set it down on the window frame. "Don't worry, I intend to help you. But I should also tell you that many folks won't be as kind as I am, and some will outright try to take what you have. I suggest that once we get you on your way, you don't stop until you get to your in-laws' place."

He grabbed my hand and shook it enthusiastically. "Oh, you bet, you bet! No way I'm stopping until I get my family somewhere safe. You can count on it." Then he turned to his wife and nearly shouted, "He's going to help us get home!"

I could see the look of relief on his wife's face, and the kids did a little happy dance together, as they chanted, "We're going to Grandma's, we're going to Grandma's, we're going to Grandma's," over and over again. I smiled, then remembered the dangers around us.

Sarah saw the look of concern on my face and turned to hush her children. "Shhhhh! Where are your manners? We hardly know this man, and you two are acting out in front of him." She turned to me and smiled briefly. "I'll keep them quiet while you two work." Yep, definitely the common sense person in this marriage.

I holstered my sidearm and got out of the truck. He grabbed my hand again and shook it, then began introductions. "Name's Dan, and that's Sarah, and Casey, and Jessica." He pointed to each of his family in turn, and then began following me around as I unpacked the jerry cans and a funnel from the car.

All the while the guy kept rattling on about where they were from and how they got here. Apparently, he'd been a graduate student at UTSA and lived on the northwest side of town, well away from the blasts. From what I understood, his car had been parked in an underground garage while he was at work, and thus protected from the EM pulse. I suspected that since it was an older model, it was less susceptible to the effects, and asked him about it.

He tapped his chin and squinted. "Hmmm, now that you mention it, there were quite a few newer cars that were inoperable. Hadn't really thought about it much."

I began filling his tank with the contents of the two jerry cans and listened as he told me more of his life story. After a minute or so, I interrupted him mid-sentence. "Dan, I'm serious about you getting your family straight to your in-laws' house without stopping. I came out from near Leakey, and from what I could tell almost the whole town was infected."

He leaned in close and whispered to me so the kids couldn't hear. "Can you keep your voice down? We don't want to scare the kids. We left town at night, and so far they've only seen them from far away. We'd like to keep it from them until we get to Sarah's parents' house."

I raised an eyebrow at that. "Well, I hate to tell you this, but there are deaders all along the highway as you head out west. The good news is that if you head back the way I came and take 41, you should have more or less smooth sailing almost all the way to Rocksprings. That little car ought to be good for a little off-roading, so if you see anything blocking the road just drive off on the shoulder and go around it. Don't stop for anything, not for people, animals, nothing. And for God's sakes, don't run over them, or you'll mess your car up and never make it there."

About that time, I heard one of the kid's yell, "Puppy!" and saw them scramble off the roof of the car, down the hood, and over to my vehicle. Before I knew it, the dog jumped out the window and ran over to the kid, and for a moment I thought I was going to have to draw down on her. Instead, the beast was licking the kid's face all over, and the kid was obviously enjoying it immensely from all the giggling going on.

The girl soon followed, and before long mom was offering the dog water from a bottle. Then she turned to me and smiled, the first real genuine smile I'd seen since I pulled up. "Beautiful dog. Is she yours?"

I shook my head. "Nope. Found her in a wrecked van a few miles back. Her owners—they weren't around. I took her with me because, well, I couldn't just leave her there."

She continued to give the dog water from the palm of her hand, pouring it from the bottle as the dog lapped it up. "She's certainly well taken care of, you can see that from her coat. Whoever owned her before must've loved her a great deal."

"Dog lover, I take it?" I asked with a grin.

Sarah nodded. "My parents raise Catahoulas, so I grew up around dogs. I'd say this one's a keeper."

It only took me a moment to decide. "Would you like to take her along with you?"

She looked at me with only the slightest bit of contempt, then caught herself. "I take it you're not a dog person?"

"No ma'am, I am—it's just that where I'm going I don't know if I could keep her safe. Besides, if you don't mind me saying, I think you and the kids could use her more than I can."

The kids immediately went into a chorus of, "Can we keep her?" and she rolled her eyes in mock annoyance. "Oh, I suppose we can keep her." A cheer went up from the peanut gallery.

Dan turned to me with concern on his face. "You sure she's going to be safe around the kids?"

I grinned. "Safe as houses. I've owned that breed before – they're good dogs, good with kids, and protective as hell." He looked to his wife for the final say, and she gave the barest of nods. That seemed to cinch it.

The kids looked over at me as I finished pouring the last drops of gas in the tank. "What's her name, mister?"

I shrugged. "She doesn't have one, so I suppose you two get to name her." They grinned, and immediately started arguing over names. "Buttercup" and "Starfire" seemed to be the two most popular choices. I decided to stay out of it.

As I threw the empty gas cans back in the bed of the truck, Dan tried to offer me money. "I feel bad about taking your gas, so at least let me pay you for it." He pushed a couple of twenties at me that he'd pulled from a wallet full of credit cards.

I chuckled and waved him off. "For one, I don't know if paper money is going to be worth anything to anyone before long. And second, this is on the house. My folks didn't raise me to take money for doing a kind turn. You can pay me back by getting your family home safe and taking good care of that dog."

He tilted his head and shook my hand. "Thanks, for everything. By the way, I never got your name."

"Nope, you didn't. It's Aidan, Aidan Sullivan. Most folks call me Sully."

One of the kids chimed in from the background. "Like the monster!" he exclaimed.

I snorted. "Just not blue and purple, but yeah."

The kid looked at me askance and squinted his eyes in feigned consternation. Then he grinned and exclaimed, "Still a cool name, even if you don't have purple fur." Then he went right back to petting the dog.

About that time, the wind shifted and I heard the dog growl menacingly. She took up a protective stance between the kids and the shoulder of the road, her gaze fixated on the treeline. I listened carefully and could hear some low moaning coming from the trees and brush, so I kept an eye on the trees while I motioned at Dan. "Take the kids to the other side of the car, and keep your eyes peeled."

I drew my Glock and started picking my way through the trees toward the moans.

———

I COULD SMELL them before I saw them. The stench was overpowering, and it was all I could do to avoid gagging and giving away my presence. I stalked forward a ways, crouched down and snuck further into the brush. Another twenty feet or so in, I saw three deaders milling about in a clearing. One was a middle-aged man in cowboy boots and a wife beater. The other two were kids.

Damn it. I could shoot the old guy without hesitation, but could I shoot these two kids? The first one couldn't have been much older than six, and he was wearing a Spongebob shirt, faded blue jeans, and a pair of Chuck Taylors. The second was a girl who was roughly ten years old, wearing bobby socks, scuffed patent leather oxfords, and a worn but service-able light blue Sunday dress. Her pale blonde hair draped across her face as she jostled past her brother, gnashing her teeth as blood dribbled down her chin.

I looked past them and saw the source of the blood. Not ten feet beyond, an overweight middle-aged woman was sprawled face down on the ground, her guts and intestines fanned out around her. There was a shotgun and a scattering of shells on the ground beside where she had fallen, and I could see that the back of her head had been blown clean away. The girl noticed me and lunged, but she stumbled and fell. I noticed then that she had a sturdy length of climbing rope around her leg, as did the boy and the man. They were all leashed to the trees that surrounded a primitive campsite, which appeared to have been hastily assembled in the clearing before me.

It didn't take long to deduce what had happened. One of the kids had probably gotten infected and turned, so the parents tied them up in the hopes that they'd get better. Then, someone else had gotten bit, maybe trying to care for the first one who had turned. Finally, another family member had gotten infected, and mom had been the last one left. Maybe she just couldn't take it, or perhaps she had sacrificed herself to feed her kids. Either way, it was tragic as hell.

I didn't have the heart to kill them, so I snuck back through the trees to where I'd left Dan and his family. I holstered my Glock before I walked over to them, and gave Dan and his wife a stern warning with my eyes that said, *Don't go back there.* Dan's wife nodded once, and then she told the kids to find something for the dog to eat.

I motioned Dan and his wife over to the cab of my truck and spoke so the kids wouldn't hear. "Don't ask me what I saw back there, because you don't want to know. Now, are you two armed?"

Dan spoke up first. "No, we don't believe in violence." His wife remained silent, and watched me carefully. I reached inside the glove box and pulled out the revolver and the box of shells I'd gotten from the truck driver the day before, then I turned and offered them to the couple. Dan raised his hands in the air and backed away a half-step. "Oh, we don't believe in guns. Please, put that away before the kids see it."

His wife, on the other hand, grabbed the pistol out of my hands, snapped the cylinder open to see if it was loaded, checked the bore, and then dumped the rounds out in her hand. She spun the cylinder and snapped it back in, then aimed off into the distance and dry fired it once to see how it functioned. And for the first time since I'd arrived, her husband stood speechless while she calmly and expertly reloaded the pistol.

Sarah turned to him and frowned. "Oh Dan, don't look so surprised. I grew up around guns, and quite frankly the kids are going to be around them a lot in the coming weeks after we get to my parent's place. You might not want them in our house, but we can't afford the luxury of pacifism anymore, not with everything that's been going on."

Dan stood there for a moment, stunned. Then, he lowered his head, resigned. "I suppose you're right. I keep thinking the way I did before the bombs fell, even though I know things have changed, maybe permanently." He turned to look at me. "Thanks, for everything."

Sarah pocketed the pistol in the back of her mom jeans and held out her hand, making confident eye contact as she did so. "Yes, thank you, Sully. You might very well have saved our lives. If you're ever out in Rocksprings, look us up. Sam and Nancy Greer are my parents, and their place is just northwest of Rocksprings on old Sonora Road. Just look for the Greer Kennel signs."

"You're welcome, and I will." I tipped my baseball cap at

them. "Dan. Sarah. Be safe." As I turned to leave, one of the kids ran up and hugged me around my leg. It was their little girl.

"Thanks for the dog, Mr. Sully. We're naming her Buttercup." Then she ran back off to where her brother was playing with the dog. I smiled, but all I could think about was the pair of little deaders who were tied up just fifty feet away.

I shook it off as I hopped in my truck, speaking to the couple through the window. "Remember, north to 41 and take that west, and you should have smooth sailing."

I waved and headed out, praying that they'd have a safe trip home.

[7]
SKIRMISHERS

WHILE I FELT great about helping Dan and Sarah and their kids, I was facing a conundrum regarding my gas situation. I didn't feel comfortable driving all the way to Austin without a few cans of gas in the back for emergencies, and that meant I'd need to gas up those cans pronto. Ingram looked like it was going to be my best bet, although with it being so close to I-10, I wasn't so sure it'd have escaped the infection.

I figured I'd just play it by ear and check the gas stations first, then try to siphon from some cars if I couldn't get it from the source. Cars seemed like the easier play, but I wanted speed over simplicity, since I'd be exposed the whole time I gassed up. Siphoning took a whole helluva lot longer than a gas pump, so if the power was on in Ingram I'd take my chances at a station.

I kept my rifle handy and made sure I had my trouble detector on full alert as I pulled into the little town. *Now, this is something strange,* I thought to myself as I rolled through the main drag. Not a soul in sight, anywhere. Huh. There wasn't a deader to be seen, nor were there any people milling about or ducking behind curtains or cars or what have you to avoid notice.

It rattled my cage a little that it was so quiet, considering the local population was roughly four times that of Leakey, but I decided that I wouldn't look a gift horse in the mouth. I circled the first gas station and convenience store I saw about three times slowly, checking inside and out for threats. Seeing nothing suspicious, I pulled up to the doors and parked so my truck door covered me in one direction, and the truck bed and camper would be covering me in another. Then I stepped out with my rifle to try the door, only to find it locked. *Shit.*

My next step was to try to jimmy the doors open. I suspected it'd be easier to use a crowbar to pry the doors apart than it would to smash the glass. Most of these gas stations used hurricane-proof glass in the doors, to make it harder for smash and grab criminals to ply their trade. That also made it safer for the night crew, should they be open 24-7 and doing business through a banker's drawer. I dug around behind the seat of the truck looking for my Fat Max demo tool, then I heard a voice behind me and to my left.

"There's an easier way to get in, you know."

I drew my sidearm and turned quickly, only to see a kid of about 11 or 12 years old staring at me from the other side of the truck window. He had a shock of unruly dirty blond hair and was wearing an old Army jacket, torn up jeans, and a pair of Doc Martens that had seen better days. I looked around to see if he was alone, but kept the pistol on him just the same. "Kind of dangerous, sneaking up on people like that."

He chewed his lip and shrugged. "Yeah, I guess so. Haven't seen too many people come through here, not since yesterday, anyway. I guess we're a little out of the way."

"You alone, kid?"

"You mean am I working with someone to distract you and steal all your stuff? No. Or, I guess yeah. Meaning I'm alone and not working with someone else."

I gave the kid a raised eyebrow. "Hmm. Say I believe you —so where are your parents?"

He rolled his eyes. "Is this where you tell me I shouldn't be out by myself, all alone during a zombie outbreak? Don't worry, it hasn't really reached us yet, so things are still pretty safe. Most people are staying indoors, working on nailing everything down. Or, they already left town."

I nodded. "Fair enough. You still didn't tell me where your parents are."

The kid threw his hands in the air. "Fine. My dad was getting drunk, the last time I saw him. And my mom works in San Antonio. I don't know when she's going to be back."

The words, "if at all" were implied in that statement. I nodded again. "Okay, I guess I'll just take you at your word. Now, you mentioned there was an easier way to get in here. Do you folks still have power?"

"Yep. So far, although it's been kind of fading in and out. Pumps still work though. I had to get some gas for my dad earlier. You just have to turn on one of the pumps from the inside."

"Okay, so how about you go inside and turn on a pump for me?"

The kid screwed his face up. "Well, about that. I may have made it harder to get in there when I went in earlier."

This time it was my turn to roll my eyes. "Seriously, kid? You're not just scamming me?"

He snickered. "Man, you really aren't the trusting sort. Here, I'll show you." He rolled under the car door and stood up next to me, then he banged on the door hard three times. Almost immediately, I heard the low moaning of two or three voices, and I saw figures shuffling from the back of the store towards the door. The kid grinned. "See, they were locked up in the back earlier, only I didn't know it. I went in there looking for supplies, like cigarettes for my dad, real food for the house, stuff like that, because the owners moved all that stuff in the back before they locked it up. So, I accidentally let them out when I was looking around for stuff."

I rubbed my chin for a minute, eyeing the deaders who were pawing at the glass and snapping their teeth at us. "How did you say you were getting in and out of this place again?"

The kid pointed up. "The roof. There's an access ladder on the other side, and I found a way to get up there that nobody knows about. So long as no one sees me, the place is all mine right now."

"Okay, so if I can go in there and kill these things, you

think you can go inside and turn a pump on for me so I can gas up and be on my way?"

The kid crossed his arms and squinted. "What's in it for me?"

Somehow, I knew he was going to say that. I pointed at the window. "Well, for starters your motherload is pretty much locked down right now, considering that those deaders in there aren't going to take too kindly to you sneaking in and out of their home. I figure you'd make a pretty handy snack for one or all three of them. Doesn't sound like the best option for a young enterprising man like yourself, to end up as chow for those freaks." I paused for effect. "Or, I could take care of your zombie problem. I help you, you help me, your old man gets his cancer sticks, and everyone lives happily ever after."

The kid acted like he was thinking about it for a moment, then he stuck out his hand. When I reached for it, he snatched it back. "Okay, but only on one condition."

"Whatever you say, kid. Hit me with it."

"All Hostess products are off limits when you go inside."

I held out my hand. "Deal. Now, show me how to get up there."

———

THE KID's route up was really simple, to be honest. If I'd have thought about it, I would have gone in that way instead of messing with the doors. Almost all of these places had some sort of roof access, and it wasn't a stretch to think that they might have external and internal access routes. We walked around the side of the building away from the street, and the kid showed me a makeshift ladder he'd made out of three of old shipping pallets. Nothing fancy, but it'd do.

After he showed me how he planned to get on the roof, I pulled my truck up to one of the pumps, just in case I needed to make a fast getaway. Then I followed the kid up to the roof. Once we were topside, he steered me to an access hatch with a huge hardened lock on it. "Tell me that you have the key for that, kid."

"Duh. Who do you think put that lock on there, one of those things downstairs?" He held up a set of keys that looked like they once belonged to a janitor. I knew immediately what I was looking at; there were a ton of keys for soda machines and other vending machines, which would make it easy to steal change and the contents of any such machine, whenever and wherever you wanted. I knew, because I'd done the same thing when I was a kid. I also saw some bump keys, and a small case that I assumed held a set of lockpicks.

I smiled and shook my head. "Well, you're just full of surprises. So, how did you like juvie, kid?"

He shrugged. "It was okay. Once the older kids figured out that I could get them anything they wanted, they pretty much left me alone."

"Sorry I asked. Why don't you go ahead and pop that thing open so I can gas up and get the hell out of here?"

He smirked at me. "Alright, alright—chillax, dude." He selected a key from his keyring and opened the hatch. "After you."

I sighed and headed down into the darkness of the store, whispering to him before I dropped. "You could have left some lights on in here."

The kid looked at me like I was nuts. "What, and attract attention to the place? No way, man. This stuff has to last me a while, at least until I can figure out a way to get it all to our trailer."

I didn't even bother gracing that with a response, thinking hard about some deader sneaking up and gnawing on my dangling legs. I lowered myself as far as I could, then I dropped down inside the place, landing on a stack of boxes and making enough noise to wake the dead, literally.

"Sorry about that!" I heard the kid whisper from above. I heard a chorus of groans and moans coming from the front of the store, so I ignored him and switched on the taclight I had mounted to the front rail of my rifle. Dead or not, I didn't want to shoot anyone if I didn't have to, so I decided to see if they'd come looking for me. Sure enough, the first one popped around the corner in short order, a girl of about 17 wearing a black and red polyester smock that said, "Traci" in cursive red letters. The predatory look in her rheumy eyes and the way she snapped her jaws at me allowed me to instantly overcome any hesitation I might have about killing these poor bastards.

"Sorry Traci, but I think you'd probably thank me for this if you could." Feeling a slight twinge or regret, I planted a round right between her eyes and she went out like a light. As she dropped I moved forward rapidly, remembering seeing three of them through the window and wanting to avoid getting boxed in. I rounded the corner toward the door where the kid had attracted them earlier, and saw one still rocking back and forth and banging lightly on the glass. I shot him in the head, and then scanned around to see where the third one had gone.

Nowhere to be found. Shit. I started to pivot around to scan my six, but before I could make the turn I felt a hand grab my shoulder with a near superhuman grip to pull me backward. So, I went with it and struck back behind me with the butt end of my rifle, making contact with the thing square in the face and knocking it back a bit. Unfortunately, it somehow managed to snag my one-point sling as it stumbled back, wrenching the rifle from my hands as it fell.

I staggered back away from it, backpedaling as I drew my Glock. The thing discarded my rifle with a clatter, then it stood and rushed toward me faster than I'd seen any of these things move so far. It was almost human-like in its movements, and definitely not the garden-variety deader I'd been accustomed to. I drew a bead on it and fired, but it zigged right and scuttled off sideways down the cooler aisle.

The kid shouted down at me from the hatch. "Are you done in there yet?"

"I'm little busy kid, so zip it!" I shouted back, scanning left and right and listening for movement, while also trying to spot it using the anti-theft mirrors in the corners of the store. Unfortunately, it was getting dark outside, so there were a lot of dark spots where the rapidly fading light outside couldn't reach.

I squatted down so it couldn't spot me and backed up to

the shelves behind me, figuring it'd have to come at me from the left or right. I waited and listened, but this thing had either been a ninja in its former life, or it was sitting just as still as I was and waiting for me to make my move. After a minute or so I got tired of waiting, and reached back to grab a can of Fix-a-Flat off the shelf. I tossed it over to the corner, just to see if the thing would react to the noise.

Sure enough, I soon heard the soft squeak of a rubber-soled shoe on linoleum. I snuck around the corner of the aisle toward the sound. As I turned the corner in a low crouch, I sliced the pie rapidly—only to find nothing there.

I caught just the flicker of a shadow cast from behind me, and did a forward roll to avoid being caught like the last time. I felt something brush my shoulder as I rolled, and came up in a shooting crouch while pivoting to face my assailant. He was almost on top of me as I fired, blowing brains and blood all over the drop ceiling in the store. The deader immediately collapsed on me, his momentum carrying me down underneath him. I was pulling myself out from under the corpse as the kid walked up and squatted down next to us.

"I was wondering what took you so long, but I guess you were humping them after you killed them. That's sick, man."

I gave the kid a dirty look and rolled the corpse over toward him, enjoying the look of betrayal on his face as he scuttled and scrambled away from the thing.

I stood up and offered him a hand. "C'mon, let's get me some gas. Daylight is burning."

———

THE KID TURNED to look back at me over his shoulder as he led the way to the front counter. "Rayden. You never asked my name. It's Rayden."

"You must be shitting me. Like the character from *Mortal Combat*? Either your parents hated you, or they were some dumb, country-ass sumbitches." He looked back at me with hurt in his eyes, which I knew was mostly for show. "Oh, c'mon—you think I'm buying that doe-eyed bullshit? Please."

"Well, at least it's better than having some stupid city-boy name. What, I bet you're probably a Tanner, or a Gavin, or a Tristan. I bet the girls must love that." He made smoochy noises at me over his shoulder. "Ohhh, Tristan, read some poetry for me." He sniggered as he jumped up and butt-vaulted the counter.

This kid was annoying the shit out of me, for sure, but I had to admit he was a funny little bastard. "It's Aidan, I'll have you know. But most folks call me Sully."

He laughed. "Oh, like Aidan is any better than Rayden. Heck, our names practically rhyme. Here you are making fun of my name, and yours is just one consonant away from mine. Not to mention that Aidan is pretty gay for a boy's name."

"Alright, alright—point taken. And you could have stopped at the rhyming bit. No need to get all personal and start talking about people's sexual preferences and what-not. I admit, my name's as goofy as yours."

He held up his hands in protest. "Whoa, whoa, whoa. I didn't say nuthin' about my name being goofy. Goofy it ain't. Chicks dig Rayden, believe me."

"I'm sure, kid. Now go flip on that pump number one so I can get the hell out of here."

As he reached for the gas pump console, the sound of multiple motorcycles surrounded us like a chorus of cicadas. I immediately squatted and duck-walked to the front so I could look out the windows. I spotted at least six headlamps circling the parking lot in the encroaching twilight.

Then, the bikes stopped moving. I saw someone dismount and head toward the front of the store, so I ran and jumped over the counter to hide. Rayden was leaning over a side counter next to the clerk's window, crushing empty cigarette cartons and other debris as he peered outside. "Aw shit, it's Cody and his goony friends."

"And just who in the hell is Cody?" I asked.

He turned to look at me. "Well, he's sort of my dad—stepdad, really. Sorry mister, but they're going to take all your stuff for sure, and they'll probably beat your ass too."

I grabbed him by the back of his Corey Feldman vintage Army jacket and hauled him off the counter, flipping him around and bringing him down as I squatted to get him at eye level with me. "You set me up kid, didn't you? Damn it!" I hit the counter next to his head, and regretted it when I saw him flinch away. I could recognize genuine fear when I saw it, and this kid wasn't afraid of me; he was afraid of the guy outside for sure, who was now banging on the window glass and yelling at us from the other side.

"Rayden, you little piece of shit! Open that gawdamn door right now, or I swear I'll beat your ass from now until doomsday when I get in there." He kicked the wall for effect. "Open this place the hell up!"

I let go of the kid and slid back against the opposite counter. "Well, he sounds like a candidate for dad of the year."

The kid slouched down to the floor with a look of resignation on his face, his shoulders slumped in defeat. "You don't know the half of it. "

"He hit you?"

"What do you think? Since mom left, suddenly I get all the attention. Not like I blame her, but she could have at least taken me with her." He paused, and looked at me. "So, what're you going to do?"

"I got parents in Austin I need to get to, and no time to screw around with this shit. Are these jokers armed?"

He nodded. "Yeah, mostly pistols, knives, brass knuckles, and the like. One or two might be carrying shotguns."

"Well, that's wonderful news." I checked my rifle to see how many rounds I had left. Almost a full magazine, so roughly 25 rounds. The Glock and Kahr were also carrying nearly full mags, and I had spares for each on me. So, I wasn't in bad shape, but a shoot-out with a half-dozen armed men was going to be a pain in the ass. I needed to come up with an equalizer, fast.

After taking a quick glance around, I grabbed a couple of bottles of lighter fluid from behind the counter and motioned to the kid. "Come on, I have a plan for taking care of these clowns. Help me, and I'll take you someplace better than this once we clear the way."

He screwed his face up at me, and I could see he was nervous, even in the dim light. Even if I couldn't see it, his voice would have betrayed his emotions to me. "You aren't going to kill him, are you? I mean, I hate him, but I don't want him dead."

"Not if I can help it, kid. But if I have to put some holes in these guys, I will. So no promises. Sorry, but I'm no victim. Question is, are you?"

He stood up and brushed himself off. "C'mon, there are some empty glass bottles in the back. You are planning on making Molotovs, right? There's some dish soap and a small gas can back there, too. I'll show you where."

[8]
RIFLE

WITHIN A FEW MINUTES, I had put together everything I'd need for a diversion and a way to even the odds. I could hear Rayden's dad yelling from outside about how he was going to beat him bloody and kill his new queer friend or some such. The guy was really starting to get on my nerves, and truth be told I didn't think I'd mind busting the proverbial cap in his ass.

Still, this kid seemed like he'd suffered enough trauma in his life. He didn't need to see his stepdad get blown away by some stranger, no matter how much of an asshole he was. So, my goal was to get these guys neutralized and get us out of here, safe, sound, and without a single shot fired. I told Rayden the plan, and he snickered as he heard me out.

The downside to this plan was that I was going to have to gas up using the siphon hose after all. The upside was that I wouldn't have to kill this kid's dad. So, all in all I'd say it had more drawbacks than benefits, but such is life. And, I was taking all the cigarettes left in the store so I could use them for bartering later. Rayden's dad could suck it.

I got everything ready and sent the kid to the front of the store. I could hear his dad yelling and cussing as I scrambled up a short aluminum stepladder the kid had found in the storage closet. We'd quickly cleared out the boxes he'd been using before, and thankfully this proved a much easier way to get to the ceiling hatch and on the roof. Since the kid's dad and his buddies were too lazy or stupid to figure out how to climb up on the roof of the gas station, chances were good we'd be able to pull this off without a hitch. Probably.

I listened carefully at the roof access opening for the kid to let his dad inside. I heard the click of the deadbolt being turned, and the change in pitch and volume of the blowhard's voice as he walked inside the place. I also heard the wet smack of meat on bone as he walloped the kid a good one.

"Damn it, boy—what the hell took you so long to open the door, and where's that feller what was helping you get inside here earlier? Don't lie to me—I saw him through the glass afore you went and hid."

Rayden spoke up, and to tell the truth I was almost ready to head down there guns blazing until I heard him speak. His voice was steady as a rock. I guess as far as getting beat by his dad went, this wasn't his first rodeo. "I was trying to find the keys to the door is all. Shit, if I had known you were going to hit me, I'd have never opened the damn door."

I heard some chuckling from the other slobs who rode in with the kid's dad. I guess they didn't like Cody much, either.

"Quit yer back-talk, or I'll hit you so hard your no-good

whore mother will feel it, wherever the hell she ran off to. Now get me some gawdamn cigarettes and that case of beer you was supposed to bring me four hours ago."

The kid chimed in again. "Hold your horses, I have it back here. But, I'm going to need some help moving this stuff. There's a bunch of beer and liquor back here, and it's going to take more than me to move it."

"Alright, you little pussy, settle yer whinin' ass down. Boys, get in here and help my good for nuthin' stepson with carrying this shit outside. Load it up in that four-by-four and we'll move it to the clubhouse." The usual bullshit that guys speak to each other when they're messing around followed, mostly just Cody's little gang arguing over who got dibs on what and all that happy horseshit.

Within moments I could hear their voices getting louder as they followed Rayden to the back of the store. It was dark, and we'd moved some boxes in the way to make it harder for his dad's goons to chase him. I slipped off the side of the building and snuck around to the doors out front, tying them off with some rope we'd found in the back as Rayden kept them distracted.

I climbed back up on the roof and waited to hear the kid give the signal.

Cody spoke up again. "By the way, what happened to that feller? You better not have let him take off with my shit, or I'll tan your ass."

"Yeah, well—he got eaten by one of those things. Why do you think it took me so long? And anyway, if you were so worried about your damn cigarettes and booze, why didn't you have one of these *bozos* to come get it? I almost got eaten too, not like you care or anything."

Bingo, that was the code word. I grabbed the length of rope that I'd tied to the ladder, then stood up and pulled the slack out, stepping on it with one foot to keep it taut. Next, I picked up one of the Molotov cocktails me and the kid had whipped up, lighting it with a pocket lighter I'd snagged from inside. Most of their bikes were bunched up right in front of the store, so I had a clear shot at them from where I stood. I chucked the bottle somewhere at the center of them all, and it made a nice large fireball as it crashed to the pavement, catching three or four bikes up in flames. I imagined that had to be hard on tires and paint, and almost felt bad about it since some of them had nice bikes. But it was just a fleeting emotion.

I heard one of the toothless wonders downstairs holler out to the rest of the crew. "Hey, what the hell is that? Looks like our bikes are on fire!" The shuffles of feet, some stuff getting knocked over, a lot of cussing and yelling, and the sounds of fists beating in futility on the front door of the store filled my ears. Soon I saw the kid's face pop up out of the trap door. I gave him a hand up, then hauled up the ladder behind him.

He slammed the door down and locked it back up tight, then turned to look at me with a mix of fear and excitement on his face. "You sure they're not getting out that front door?"

"Not for a while, kid. Now let's haul ass before they figure out a way to bust through that front door glass."

I was no sailor, but I knew how to tie a decent knot; that

rope would hold them inside, and since there was a security plate on the door, there was no way they were going to cut it from the inside. Until they smashed through that hurricane glass, they were stuck. Even so, I wasn't counting on them taking long to get through it, and sent the kid on ahead to the truck while I started shooting gas tanks on the bikes that hadn't gotten caught up in the fire. Then, I threw the other two Molotovs at the bikes that weren't yet on fire and hauled ass to the truck with the sounds of gunfire and breaking glass erupting from behind me.

"Won't be long before they get out of there and steal a car to chase us, kid. With it being dark, we need a place to hole up. Got any ideas?"

"Yeah, just head out toward Kerrville and turn right on 98. We can hide out on the other side of the lake, I got a place won't no one find us, at least not till morning."

———

I FOLLOWED the kid's directions and parked in what looked like empty park land, hidden in a thicket of trees on the south side of Nimitz Lake. I took the cab of the truck and let him sleep on my camping mattress in the back, and I kept one eye open as I tried to catch a few winks without letting those morons from back at the gas station sneak up on us and catch us flat footed. After midnight I realized that we'd lost them, at least for the moment, and managed to get a few hours of rest.

I woke up before sunup and roused the kid from sleep. We shared a breakfast of water, Power Bars, and jerky in silence, then I pulled out my atlas and a small flashlight and consulted with him as we ate. "Rayden, I'd like to avoid Kerrville if possible. It's not a big town, but I'm worried about running into large groups of infected. How Ingram dodged that bullet, I don't know, but I'm assuming Kerrville is going to be worse."

He nodded and cleared his throat. "Shit, are you asking me for directions? I can't even drive yet, man."

"Good point." I chewed my lip and looked over the map some more. "Well, I was planning on taking back roads to Austin, but I guess we'll just have to plow straight through Kerrville. The next hurdle will be Fredericksburg, but we'll cross that bridge when we get to it." I put the atlas up, reloaded all my mags, and we headed out.

As we drove into town the sun was starting to come up, and soon we could see smoke billowing skyward all over the city. I'd smelled it the night before, but now we could see thick clouds of it floating up from fires that were raging in various buildings and businesses all across town. We were in the city limits proper already, and it wasn't too long before we started seeing deaders shuffling around the area. They were obviously attracted to sound, and before long we had them coming at us from all directions as I drove up the street to the bridge crossing the Guadalupe River. I just managed to dodge a few of them, but was forced to run a couple over at low speed in order to make the bridge.

Once we were on the bridge, it was more a matter of dodging cars than people to get through. After leaving the bridge we continued north at a decent pace, dodging larger groups of deaders and more than a few car accidents and abandoned vehicles. We passed the courthouse, which was a pile of smoldering embers, and on through downtown Kerrville. There were numerous restaurants and other businesses along this road, and more often than not we saw deaders milling about inside, banging on windows or crawling over corpses as they responded to the sound of the truck as it passed by.

This place was a ghost town, or it would have been if it weren't for the hundreds upon hundreds of deaders that still occupied its streets. I continued to zig zag down the road until we were nearly out of town and in sight of the intersection with I-10.

The whole overpass had been taken out, and in its place was a massive pile-up of charred and smoking cars, trucks, tractor-trailers, and debris. As I slowed down and we drove closer, I could see the remnants of an airliner fuselage in the debris, as well as a piece of a wing that was sticking out of a Dairy Queen like a discarded toy.

Rayden gaped at the carnage and whistled out one long, high note. "Holy shit. I ain't never seen anything like this. Not in my whole life."

I shook off the jitters starting to sneak up on me and tried to stay on task. "Yeah, it's pretty bad. The real problem for us though is getting through this mess." I scanned left and right as we got closer to the wreckage, picking out a clear path to the right. "I'm going to head down that way and see if there's a place we can cross the highway. Keep your eyes peeled for trouble."

We were forced to drive on the shoulder as I headed east, following the merge lane that once took traffic from 16 onto I-10. Again, there were abandoned cars and trucks all along the road clogging the way, and many of them were occupied by the dead—some of them less dead than others. Thankfully, about 100 yards east we were able to drive down a rain culvert and cross under the highway to the other side. As we passed the westbound side of the highway, I saw a small group of adults huddled under the overpass, warming themselves around a small fire. They looked haggard, dirty, and lost. I drove on despite their cries for help.

Rayden shook my arm. "You ain't going to stop?"

"Can't save everyone, kid. If I tried, you and me would be dead before the day was out. Look around you. This is a zombie apocalypse, true shit hitting the fan, the end of the world as we know it scenario. And it's only going to get worse. My goal is to get to my folks, head back out to the boonies, and then do what I can for any survivors who might be holed up around my area. Doesn't mean I don't want to help those folks, but right now the risk factor is too high."

He nodded. "I guess you're right. Still don't seem fair, though."

"It isn't, kid. It damned sure isn't."

———

As I PULLED BACK onto the highway, I reflected on the fact that I was feeling copacetic as hell. I kept waiting for another panic attack to hit, but they never came. I honestly didn't know if that meant I was broken, or fixed. Regardless, the fact that it took the onset of a zombie apocalypse to get my head right certainly said something about the nature of my psychological make-up, that was for sure. If things ever got back to normal, I'd have to get a t-shirt made that said, "Killing Zombies Saved My Brain" or something like that. Then again, if things ever got back to normal I'd probably start losing my shit again, too.

About ten miles down the road we came across a sight for sore eyes. It was a gasoline tanker, left right there in the middle of the road, without a soul around in sight. I stopped the truck a ways down the road and pulled out my binos, scoping the area out for a good ten minutes before we drove up on it slow and easy.

There was zero movement in the cab or around the vehicle, nor could I see anything moving in the juniper trees and live oaks off to either side of the road. Vegetation was sparse along this stretch of highway, but it didn't mean there couldn't be someone out there waiting in ambush, so I asked Rayden if he knew how to shoot a rifle.

"Does a bear shit in the woods? I mean, I never shot one like yours, but yeah, I can shoot."

"Well, that's good, because we're almost out of gas and I'm going to need to find a way to get some fuel out of this tanker so we don't end up stranded like every other dumbass on this road. That means I'm going to need you to pull overwatch while I'm gassing up the truck."

He grinned. "Just like *Call of Duty*. Hell yes!"

"Hang on there, Jack Mitchell. This ain't like a

videogame, not at all. There's no save game to go back to, no extra lives, and no setting the game to easy mode to make the baddies easier to frag. I need you to be serious about this, because I'm going to be counting on you to keep my ass alive if something goes wrong."

He sized me up and laughed. "Look around, man. There's no one out here for miles! What could go wrong?"

"Everything. So I want you on the roof of this truck with that rifle and the binos, scanning the area and shooting anything that moves and looks hostile. If it's a deader, head-shots only. If it looks human, fire a warning shot at its feet first. I'll come running if I hear you fire, anyway." I showed him how to operate the rifle and chambered a round. "Got it?"

"Got it!" He grabbed the rifle and jumped out of the cab. I sighed and prayed that I wasn't making a mistake, and grabbed the gas cans out of the back along with the siphon hose. I stalked up to the cab of the semi with the gas cans in one hand, using the siphon hose as a carrying handle, with my Glock in the other hand. The cab was empty and had the keys in it. I turned the key and sure enough, the truck had run out of fuel. Since most of these trucks ran local routes, carrying enough diesel to drive up to 1,000 miles, I figured this guy must've been in a hurry when he'd taken off without filling up.

I clambered up on the tanker and began checking the fuel levels using the access ports on top. There were four separate tanks from what I could tell, and the first two I opened were too low for the hose to reach. I struck gold on the third tank; it was almost full. It took a few minutes to siphon enough gas to fill each can, then I had to walk back to the truck and empty them in the tank. I did this another time, topping the truck off, then I went back with that can a third time to fill it once more.

Just as I was putting the cap back on the can, I heard Rayden holler at me from the truck. "Um, I think you're going to want to see this!"

"Hang on, I'm coming," I called back.

"Yeah, well, I think you'd better hurry. I mean hurry, hurry. I mean like get your ass over here right now, man!"

I stood up and looked over where the kid was looking. There was a herd of about a dozen or so of them coming out of the trees from the direction of Kerrville. What made them wander out this way was anyone's guess, but I suspected they'd been in pursuit of someone on foot who decided to take their chances in the sticks instead of staying in town. Probably the sound of my exhaust had attracted them to us.

They were moving pretty slow, and fact was we had plenty of time to load up and get away. Still, I thought this might be a good time to let the kid get used to killing these things. It was tough love, but it might have saved his life later.

"I'm still trying to fill up this can!" I hollered from the top of the tanker. "You have the rifle, so start taking them out to give us some more time while I finish up!" I feigned urgency but really I wasn't all that concerned. I didn't see any fast ones in the bunch, and in my experience you could dodge these things on foot without breaking a sweat. I fiddled with the siphon hose and waited to see what he would do.

The crack of the rifle sounded off, and I saw one drop out of my peripheral vision. Turned out the kid was a decent shot after all. He fired again nine more times, and seven of those nine times resulted in stopping a deader in their tracks. Their second death, I supposed. Whatever. All I knew was that I could rely on the kid in a pinch, and that's what mattered. I gathered up the siphon hose and can, snapped the lid back down on the tank in case we needed to come back for more later, and moseyed on over to the truck.

"Is that all of them?" I asked as I placed the can and siphon hose in the bed of the truck.

He nodded, and kept scanning the area. "I think so. I see some movement way out there, but I think we have time. Don't want to waste anymore ammo."

"Alright, good job, kid. Come on down and let's get out of here." He climbed down and handed me the rifle, and I pulled the magazine and popped in a fresh one before I hopped in the driver's seat. I looked over at Rayden as he climbed in, and could see he was a bit conflicted about what had just happened. "Those the first ones you killed?"

"Yeah. It felt kind of weird, you know? I mean, I know they're not alive anymore—I seen one of Cody's guys come back, so I know they're dead—but it still made me a little queasy."

"Well, that just means you're human. And frankly, I don't know what causes those things to come back from the dead, and I don't know whether or not they remember anything or if they're even remotely human. What I do know is that it's them or us, so you can rest easy knowing you did well."

The kid kind of blushed at what I said. I figured he didn't know how to take praise, which was to be expected. I acted like I didn't notice, and took off down the road for Fredericksburg and whatever awaited us there. For the next few miles Rayden just stared out the window at nothing. Guess there wasn't anything else to be said about it. Killing's never easy for a sane person, even when the things you're killing are already dead. He'd get used to it, or he'd be dead soon as well, and nothing else I could say would make it any easier.

[9]
REGIMENT

As we came into Fredericksburg, we got a helluva surprise. Just before the airport, the road was blocked by several metal storage containers that were placed end to end across the asphalt. They stretched from the fenceline on one side to the fenceline on the other, with a gap between the middle two that was just big enough for a large truck to pull through. That gap appeared to be blocked by a moving truck that someone had welded to a cattle gate, so the gate blocked the space between the bumper and the ground.

On top of the shipping containers they'd stacked sandbags six feet high, and I immediately noticed that shooting ports were built into the wall on either side. I couldn't see if anyone had a bead on us, but I assumed they did. I slowed down to see whether the folks who put it up might be friendlies or hostiles, then heard someone shout at us over a loudspeaker from the direction of the road block.

"This is Lieutenant Thomas Wheeler of the Texas National Guard! We have snipers targeting your vehicle, and they will disable your vehicle should you try to flee. You are commanded to drive your vehicle up to the blockade and park, then follow our instructions to the letter. Any deviation from these instructions will be interpreted as a hostile action, and deadly force will be used. Please proceed forward at no greater than five miles an hour, park, and await instructions."

"Well shit," I declared to no one in particular. They could have been bluffing, but I didn't feel like risking getting my engine block blown to hell. Not to mention getting our asses shot off to boot. I put the truck in gear and inched up to the road block.

The kid looked at me with contempt. "Aw man, you're actually listening to this guy? How do you know they're not going to shoot us and take all our stuff? Haven't you ever watched any of the *Road Warrior* movies?"

I kept my eyes on the makeshift wall and gate ahead as I responded to his comments. "I am, I don't, and I have, every last one, even that last shitty one that had no plot. Fact is, if they do have snipers on us we'd be shot before we turned the truck around. Best that we take our chances here and see what is what. Besides, aren't you even a little curious to find out if the Guard or other branches of the military are getting this mess under control?"

He shrugged. "I guess. But to me it looks like this is just another bunch of people who want to boss everyone else around for no good reason."

"You're probably right on the money with that observation, but let's hope that these folks are on the up and up. Put your hands up where they can see them." Rayden did as he was told, and as we pulled up to the gate, the guy with the bullhorn provided instructions for us to exit the vehicle with our hands in the open. As we did, the moving truck was pulled back a few meters, and two National Guardsman and a sheriff's deputy came out from behind the roadblock with guns drawn. I noted that the cop had a Remington 870 pump, and the Guardsmen carried M4's. The uniforms and gear loadout all looked legit, so I decided to keep playing along in the hopes of getting some decent intel.

The cop spoke first, which I thought was weird. But considering that the whole deal basically constituted using military force against civilians, I supposed it made sense that they'd try to give the impression that local law enforcement was still in charge. "Arms out to your sides, so we can search you."

We did as instructed, and the soldiers walked up and searched us both. They took my Glock and my Bowie knife, but left me my combat folder. I guessed they were making small concessions to make it look like they weren't really instituting martial law.

I was quickly tiring of the whole charade, so I decided to try to get some info and see if they'd release us. "Officer, we're just passing through on our way to go get my parents." I tilted my head at Rayden, "His grandparents, from Austin. We've seen a lot on the way here—"

"The way here from where?" The cop went into interrogation mode almost on cue, which I took as a bad sign.

"From around Leakey. My folks have a ranch out there."

He grunted. "Leakey was overrun by the infected. Got a distress call from their dispatch 'bout two weeks ago. Far as we know, none of them survived. So, either you're lying, or you're damned lucky."

I did my best "aw shucks" routine to try to get him to relax and see us as no threat. "Lucky. I started driving to Leakey and saw a whole herd of those things coming up the road. So I turned around and headed north to 41. It was more or less clear sailing until we got to Kerrville."

He looked distraught at the mention of Kerrville. "Yeah, Kerrville. Bad news, that. You see any survivors there?"

"A few, under the overpass on the I-10 east of town. We didn't stop; I have the boy's safety to think of, you know."

The officer gave me a look that said I was chickenshit, then caught himself. "Yeah, well. Can't say I blame you. Folks are desperate. Heard talk of roving bands of looters, gangs burning homes, rape—you name it. Probably better off keeping to yourself, that's for sure." He hollered over to the soldiers, who were now searching through my truck. "What'd you find?"

"A rifle and a lot of ammo. Some camping gear, food, and water. The usual." The soldiers held up my rifle and an ammo can to show the deputy.

He answered back to the soldiers. "Tag it and take it to HQ, along with his sidearms." He turned back to us and waved in dismissal. "You two can relax." He held out his hand to me, and I noticed that his smile didn't reach his eyes. "My name's Deputy Carson, and you're fortunate to have stumbled on one of the only safe zones in the Texas Hill Country. The sheriff and the Guardsmen that the governor sent down here managed to secure a safe zone from the downtown area to the high school, which is where we have most of the town safely sequestered."

"Sequestered? I hope you don't mind me asking, but you are intending to let us go on our way, right?" I tried to put as much obsequiousness into my words as I could muster, but frankly I was a little hacked off at the whole situation.

He held his hands up and smirked a little. "Now, now—I know how this looks, what with us taking your guns and all. But you can understand that we can't have people walking around town armed, not with the way things are, and especially not strangers. Soon as the captain hears your story and decides you can go, I'm sure you'll be on your way." He turned to one of the soldiers. "Hey Rizzo, can you escort these two—" he glanced over at me. "What were your names again?"

"John Sullivan, and this is James, my son."

The look on his face told me he wasn't buying it, but that it wasn't his problem, either. I didn't have any ID on me anyway, so there'd be no way to check my story, not without a working computer system and Internet—which I somehow doubted they had. "Like I was saying, can you escort Mr. Sullivan and his son to HQ, and get them a hot meal before they see the commander?"

"Sure thing, deputy." He gestured that we should follow him. "I'll have to drive your vehicle, company commander's orders. Kid can ride in the back."

I decided to play along, since there were no other options at the moment and there was no way I was going to risk getting shot over nothing. As we pulled through the gate, I could see the LT who had hollered at us with the bullhorn on top of the wall, along with two guys in sniper's nests hidden behind a wall of sandbags. Guess I'd made the right call.

The ride to the HQ, which turned out to be the high school, was short and uneventful. I tried to pump Rizzo for info on the way over, but he was tight-lipped on the situation. When we pulled up to the front of the high school he stopped my truck and told us to get out. "I'll park your vehicle in the motor pool, and your keys will be stored securely along with your weapons and ammo. I'll come back to have you sign for them, and you'll get them back when the commander says you can leave."

"How long do you think that'll be?" I asked, with only a slight bit of concern in my voice.

"Oh, a day at most. Until then, just head through those doors and ask for Corporal Parker, she'll get you squared away." He started to drive off, and I tapped on the door to get him to stop.

"You mind if I get our stuff from the back?"

He waved me off. "Oh, you won't need it. They have everything you'll need. Cots, blankets, and food. And a place to take a hot shower, too. I imagine you two could use a bath, being on the road and all. So, enjoy it, and I'll see you in a few." He drove off without a wave or a howdy-do. Asshole.

I turned to Rayden. "Well kid, looks like we're staying the night."

He smirked, hacked up some snot from the back of his throat, and spat on the sidewalk. "Ya think?"

———

TRUE TO RIZZO'S WORD, Corporal Parker hooked us up with some hot food and a cot once we checked in at the makeshift HQ desk they'd set up. She was a short, stocky little country girl with light brown hair, freckles dotting her cheeks, and an upbeat country attitude that said, "Society might be breaking down all around us, but I've chosen to ignore it and pretend things are just peachy-keen!" She gave us our room assignment and then escorted us partway down the hall to the mess, where she sent us on our way with a perky smile, little to no eye contact, and a nervous wave goodbye. Suddenly, I felt *so* much better about our predicament.

At first glance it looked like things were pretty sedate around the place, at least until they took us to the cafeteria. I realized there that they had quite a sizable group of people holed up in here. The cafeteria was full of families, the elderly, and people of all ages and types, most of them looking shell-shocked and confused. We got our food and sat down at a table with an elderly woman dressed in a flower print shirt, mom jeans, and tennis shoes. She wore a ball cap that said "I'm A Virgin" in large letters. Underneath that in small type it said, "(but this is an old hat)."

She held out her hand as we sat down, and I took it as introductions were made all around. "I'm John and this is my son, James."

She gave me a wry smile. "Barbara Baumgartner. Friends call me Bibi. I take it you two aren't from around here?"

"No ma'am, we just drove in from around Leakey."

She screwed up her face as if wondering whether she should tell us whatever it was she was thinking. I could tell she was going to spill anyway; she looked like the type who said whatever was on her mind regardless of the consequences. She looked at Rayden. "I have a grandson about your age. Full of piss and vinegar, that boy. Looks a lot like you. And if you're this guy's son, I'm a horse's ass."

Rayden thought that was pretty funny, and he shot a little milk out of his nose as he expressed his mirth. She nodded and turned to me. "Uh-huh, thought so. I take it you were on your way out of wherever the hell you came from, and decided to help this young man out. No need to explain, I can read people pretty well. Seventy-three years on this earth will do that for you."

She looked me up and down, appraising me much more closely than I was comfortable with. "You're ex-military. I can tell by the way you sit. My Lou was a military man, gave three decades of his life to the Navy. Retired and we settled back here in my hometown so we could be near my family. He volunteered at the Nimitz museum. Gave tours to the visitors from Austin and Dallas. A good man, my Lou. He'd never have put up with this shit, that's for sure."

I decided to take that opportunity to get a word in edgewise and find out more about the town and what was going on here. "Mrs. Baumgartner, if you don't mind me asking, just what sort of shit are you referring to?"

She sat back in her chair and gestured like a game show model showing off a new car to the contestants. "Well, just look around you and marvel at what our good sheriff and that two-bit weekend warrior have cooked up to keep us all safe." She made quotation marks with her fingers as she said the word "safe." "Has us all locked up here in this school like cattle, just waiting to be slaughtered. Oh, Lou would have raised holy hell, yes he would have."

"But Mrs. Baumgartner—"

She cut me off mid-sentence. "That'll be enough of that 'misses' crap. Call me Bibi."

"Bibi it is, then. What do you mean when you say you're all just waiting to be slaughtered?"

She looked around a bit, then leaned in close with her elbows on the table. On cue, Rayden and I likewise leaned in. "Now, you listen to me and you listen good. These aren't just the ravings of some crazy old widow. I'm as sharp as the day I received my doctorate from A&M, and let me tell you that you two aren't safe here! The last two families that came in from out of town disappeared, and no one knows what happened to them."

I furrowed my brow and replied. "What makes you think

they disappeared? I mean, the sheriff and the commander might have just let them leave."

She cocked an eyebrow at us and chuckled. "Oh, so then tell me why their vehicles are still here? Auggie works down in the motor pool—he's our local mechanic, so he's one of the first ones they pressed into service when they rolled into town after the bombs fell. Auggie sees all the vehicles they bring in, as he works right down there where they lock up all the Hummers and personnel carriers. And I'm telling you that those people vanished, but Auggie says their cars are still parked down there in the motor pool with all the rest."

"Is there any way you can get me a chance to speak with this Auggie guy?"

She shook her head. "I don't really think you have time for all that. It wasn't but the same night those folks came in that they disappeared. I'm telling you that you need to get out of here, and pronto. Else you two might end up as gone as the rest of them."

I rubbed my chin, ready to pose another question, when she suddenly stood up and grabbed her tray. "Well, nice speaking with you boys, but I promised to do some sewing for the Johnson family, and after that me and some of the girls are meeting for a game of bridge." She winked at me and scurried off as a soldier walked up to our table.

"Commander wants to see you as soon as you finish your meals and get settled. Head up to where you signed in at intake and tell them you're there to see Captain Hillis."

———

THE WAIT TO see the commander took no time at all. We were soon ushered into what looked like a principal's office, where a trim and fit-looking man with light hair and glasses sat behind a desk reading what looked like mission status reports. He stacked and shuffled them neatly, tucking them inside a manila folder as we walked in. Then he looked us up and down for moment before gesturing to a pair of chairs in front of the desk.

"Please, have a seat. My name is Captain Paul Hillis of the 136th Military Police Battalion out of Tyler. We've been assigned here by request of the governor to aid local law enforcement and set up safe zones in the Texas Hill Country, where we can provide increasing support and protection to the people of this and the surrounding counties." The whole thing sounded like a speech that he'd memorized and practiced in the mirror a few times. He reminded me of a politician. I had him pegged as a cake eater from the moment he opened his mouth.

"John Sullivan, and this is my son, James." I gestured at Rayden, and he gave a smart-assed two-fingered salute. "If you don't mind me asking, sir, why do you have all the local residents sequestered here at the high school?"

He gave me a stern look as he replied. "Why, to protect them, of course. You carry yourself like a soldier, son. Did you serve?" I nodded. "Well, then you understand the importance of maintaining order under these conditions. We're still under threat of further nuclear attack, we're facing mass looting across the state, panic has erupted everywhere there are sizable populations of people left alive, and I'm certain I don't have to explain the situation with the infected. Whether it's a biological agent, chemical toxin, or some other unknown weapon, we aren't certain. But what we do know is that it's contagious, and we cannot let it spread among the local population. It has a 100 percent transmission rate upon exposure, so the safest place these people can be is here under our protection."

"100 percent? So why didn't you put us under quarantine when we came in?"

At that, a look crossed his face that told me he was hiding something. It quickly passed and his expression reverted to the baby-kissing politician once more. "If either of you were infected, we'd have known of it immediately. Once you contract the contagion, the transformation is almost immediate."

I cleared my throat, because I was about to stir up some shit and wanted to be sure he heard me. "You do realize that this contagion is reanimating corpses, correct?"

The captain sat back in his chair with his hands on the edge of his desk. He fixed me with a look that clearly said he'd underestimated what I knew. "So, you've see this happen?"

I waved his comment away. "No, but several of the 'infected' that I've had to put down were missing so many body parts that there was no way they could've survived their injuries. I have yet to see a living person turn, so I assumed that it only affected the dead."

He nodded. "Partially true. The infected have a toxin in their saliva that will kill within hours once it enters the bloodstream. Once the newly infected's heart stops beating, that's when they turn into those creatures you've seen."

"Huh. That gives me something to think about as we continue on into Austin. I'm sure your people told you that we're on our way to bring my parents back to the Hill Country?"

He nodded. "I assure you, we won't hold you up. However, it is policy that we do not allow anyone in or out of the safe zone after 5 pm. It looks like you two will be spending the night as our guests. In the morning, your equipment, weapons, and vehicle will be returned to you, and you can be on your way."

"That's good to know, sir."

"Now, I have some reports to review before evening chow, but I've arranged for Corporal Parker to place you in our overflow area, since the main living area in the gym is at capacity. It's actually fortunate that you've come to us now, since you'll only be sharing the room with a few other people."

I stood up and extended my hand. "Thanks, Captain. We won't be a bother while we're here." I noticed that Captain HIllis hesitated slightly before standing and shaking hands with me. I filed it away for future reference.

His eyes narrowed slightly as he spoke. "I'm counting on it. Good evening, gentlemen."

I motioned for Rayden to exit the office, then followed him out and shut the door behind me. He immediately grabbed my arm and began whispering in my ear. "Sully, I don't trust that guy—"

I pulled him into an open doorway, covering his mouth lightly with my free hand. "Not here. Wait until I'm certain we're alone." I checked the hall before we exited the room, and we headed back to the front desk where Corporal Parker waited to guide us to our assigned quarters. I had a feeling it was going to be one hell of an interesting night.

[10]
CHAOS

SINCE WE'D JUST EATEN EARLIER, we passed on the
evening meal. Instead of heading back to the chow hall, we
followed the directions Parker had given us and made a
beeline for our "quarters," which turned out to be a small
classroom upstairs. Obviously it had been set up in a hurry,
because all the desks and chairs had merely been pushed out
of the way, making room for a few cots and some sleeping
bags.

I quickly checked the hall to make sure no one was
listening in on us, then did a quick visual check of the room
for cameras and wires. Once I felt satisfied that no one was
eavesdropping, I pulled Rayden over to the cots and sat
down, taking a moment to mull over what I was going to say. I
could tell by the look on his face that he was a little worried,
but I didn't think it'd do to mince words with him.

I just put it out there.

"I think we may be well and truly screwed here, kid."

Rayden chewed his lip and scowled. "Man, I should have stayed in Ingram. At least with Cody and his dickhead buddies, I knew what I was in for. Here, all I know is that these people have a seriously creepy vibe going on, but I have no idea what's coming. Feels like I'm in a horror film or something, where you know something bad is going to happen, but you don't know what." He shivered like a wet dog and wrapped his arms around himself as his eyes darted around the room.

I punched him lightly on the knee and smiled in a way that I hoped was reassuring. "I know how you feel, but trust me, I've been in worse situations than this. That's why we're not spending the night; in fact, we're going to sneak out as soon as it gets dark around here."

The kid perked up at that. "Alright, so what's the plan?"

"Well, I don't know if you noticed, but the second floor roof is just outside this window. Should make it easy to sneak out of here. So as soon as it's dark I'm going to go find my gear, and you're going to wait here in case anyone comes by while I'm gone. Once I get my stuff and locate the truck, I'll come back to get you."

He shook his head and frowned. "I don't know if I like the idea of being left by myself. What if they come to take me away while you're gone?"

"I doubt they'll do anything to us unless we're together, so just tell them I went to the bathroom and stall until I get back. Deal?"

"I guess so. But don't leave me here with these people, no matter what. I don't like it here—this place creeps me out."

"Yeah, me too. I won't leave you here, kid. We made a deal, and I'll see it through." I smiled again, this time with more conviction. "Although you have to admit, this is a helluva lot safer than Ingram."

He smiled back, but his heart obviously wasn't in it. "Yeah, I'd say that's a matter of opinion. I bet those people who disappeared don't think so."

"Don't worry, kid. In a few hours we'll be out of here and on our way to Austin."

He dropped back on the cot and tucked his hands under his head. "I am *sooooo* looking forward to it."

———

LATER THAT EVENING two more people were brought into the room, a mother and who I assumed was her child. Strangely, they were brought in by two armed soldiers; I chalked that up to the fact that they were illegals. I figured they hadn't met anyone around here who spoke Spanish, so I started up a conversation with the mom to pass the time and put her at ease.

She seemed nervous at first, but eventually she opened up to me. Her name was Lupita, and she told me they'd crossed the border together before the outbreak, and that she'd come to Fredericksburg to work for a bed and breakfast service doing house work. Her daughter's name was Elena, and she spent most of our conversation hiding behind her mother's leg, at least until Rayden pulled out some licorice whips.

"Hey, where'd that come from?" I asked.

"Duh, the convenience store. You don't think I went in there just to get Cody his beer and cigarettes, do you?" He gave me the universal "adults are so stupid" look that all kids master by the time they hit puberty, and handed Elena two licorice strings, which she took with a shy smile.

"Nice to know you've been holding out on me all this time. Also nice to know you're smart enough not to bring chocolate with you on a road trip."

He laughed. "You kidding? That's the first thing I ate."

"See if I give you any more jerky once we get our shit back."

He rolled his eyes. "You can keep it. I have enough candy to last me a few more days."

"Whatever, kid. Enjoy it while it lasts, because you may not be able to get any for a while. I have a feeling that the trucking industry is going to be out of commission for a good long time, so you'd better get used to eating jerky." He shrugged, and I turned back to speak with Lupita. I noticed that she kept glancing out the window and scanning the skyline outside. I asked her in Spanish if anything was wrong.

In response she grabbed me and took me aside, away from where her daughter and Rayden were playing. *"El cucuy, viene en la noche! Por favor, usted debe salir y nos llevará con usted!"*

Rayden perked up and spoke to me over his shoulder. "She sounds upset. What's she saying to you?"

I shook my head. "Something about a monster that comes at night. She's asking me to leave and take them with us." I continued to try to get more information out of her, but all I could get her to tell me was that the guards wouldn't let them leave, that a dark figure had come the night before and took some people out of the room.

I figured that if it was real it was probably soldiers, and if it wasn't she was in shock and having nightmares. I tried to calm her down, but it was no use. Eventually she gave me a frustrated look and grabbed Elena, then sat on a cot on the other side of the room.

"What'd you say to piss her off?" Rayden asked.

"Nothing. Maybe she's just scared that the soldiers are going to take her and Elena to jail or something. She says a dark figure came in the room last night and grabbed some people. I think it may have been the soldiers moving people around." I glanced outside and noticed that it was finally fully dark. "At any rate, it's none of our concern. We just need to grab our gear and get the hell out of here."

Rayden looked at me like I was the biggest asshole in the world. "Yeah, but if something really is going on, you're not just going to leave them here, are you?"

"Not my monkeys, not my circus, kid. Believe me, I would if I could, but we're barely going to have room for my folks on the way back. Besides, I'd feel terrible taking these people out of here and putting them in harm's way. Things are only going to get hairier and scarier the closer we get to Austin, and I'm going to have my hands full just keeping an eye on you."

He gave me the evil eye. "That's cold, man."

"That's survival, kid. I learned in Afghanistan that you

can't save everyone, no matter how much you want to or how hard you try."

"Maybe so, but it's still messed up."

I shrugged. "You'll get no arguments on that point from me, but that's just life. The sooner you learn to accept it, the better."

He ignored me and rolled over on his cot. I decided to leave him to his thoughts, which were likely filled with disillusionment. Wouldn't be the first time I'd let someone down, and it wouldn't be the last. My main concern was getting us out and long gone before the local law and those Guard troops knew we'd disappeared, then I'd focus on rescuing my parents. Outside of that, all other concerns would be secondary, at least until I had us all safe and sound back at the ranch.

I tried to get Rayden's attention to give him a few final instructions, but he pretended to be asleep. Since the kid was giving me the silent treatment, there was nothing else to do but wait. I fluffed my pillow, laid my head back on the cot, and waited for lights out. After that, the black ops shit would commence.

———

JUST AS I SUSPECTED, at 10 pm sharp a soldier came by to check on us and turn the lights out. After he left I heard him messing around with the door, so I waited for a few minutes and then snuck over to whisper in Rayden's ear. "Kid, keep your eyes peeled. If anything happens while I'm gone, you beat feet out of here, you hear me? Head down to the gymnasium and hide there. If I come back and you're gone, I'll come get you down there. Got it?"

He paused before replying. "Yeah, I got it."

"Good. I'll be back before you know it."

I gave him a pat on the shoulder and tiptoed over to the window, then I popped it open and slipped out into the night. It was darker than hell outside, and from what I could tell the place was running on generators for most of the settlement's power. That meant minimal lighting in non-mission critical areas, and it also meant that the sound would help muffle my movements.

I crawled along the wall and climbed down a drain pipe, then crept around the place until I figured out where the HQ area was in relation to the room they'd put us in. After that, it was just a matter of sneaking and peeking in a few windows to find where they'd stashed our stuff. I used my multi-tool to get the window open and rifled through the room until I found my ammo and knife.

The firearms were a bit more of a hassle, as I had to jimmy a few storage cabinets until I found what I was looking for. The assholes hadn't even tagged my shit, which told me they had no intention of returning any of it. I decided that I'd best find my vehicle and get us the hell out of here before we experienced firsthand what was really going on in this place.

It didn't take much to sneak past the guards on patrol. They were sloppy and not at all concerned with keeping anyone in the place. I headed down to the parking lot where Bibi had said the cars were kept, and sure enough my baby was parked in the back. There was only one guard on duty, so I snuck up behind him and choked him out. I gagged him and tied him up, leaving him in the back of a Hummer for the next shift to find him in the morning.

After that, it was a matter of pulling my taillight's fuse to keep the headlights off as I pulled out of the place. I only had to drive a few blocks to find the fence perimeter they'd set up; once there I parked the truck in someone's driveway near the fence line, back behind the house where no one would see it. Later I planned to use my bolt cutters to clip a hole in the fence and get us the hell out of there, right after I went back for Rayden.

I checked my watch; it was roughly 30 minutes past midnight. Plenty of time to jog back to the high school, get Rayden, and be gone before dawn. I headed back over, being mindful of patrols, especially since they were probably rolling with night vision on blackout lights. I managed to evade the only patrol I saw and snuck around the back of the high school where I had climbed down a few hours before.

Just as I climbed back on the rooftop that led to the room we'd been assigned, I saw a shadow moving away from the window at high speed. It looked like a man, but I'd never seen anything on two legs move that fast before. It looked as though it might have been carrying something in its arms, but I couldn't be sure in the dark. I followed it with my eyes, watching it jump off the roof. It landed upright and continued on without pause, speeding in a southwesterly direction in the span of a few seconds. Momentarily stunned, I ran back over to our room, frightened of what I might find inside, hoping it was just my eyes playing tricks on me.

Sure enough, it wasn't anything I'd have wanted to see. Lupita was sprawled on the ground, her neck twisted at an odd angle. My eyes searched the room, but the kids were nowhere to be seen. I stuck my head inside and started calling out in the lowest voice I could for Rayden but got no answer, so I climbed inside to see if he'd run off like I told him to.

I was just about to go looking for him in the mess when I heard some moaning off to one side of the room. I ran over and found the kid lying in a tangle of plastic school chairs, battered but basically unhurt. He was dazed, but as he came around he described what had happened.

"Just a couple of minutes ago, I got up to look for you out the window and saw something outside. I thought it was you and went to open the window. Then I saw what it was and went to wake up Lupita and Elena so we could get the hell out of here. She was already awake, but I couldn't get her to move. She just laid there whimpering and holding on to her little girl. So, I ran to the door to get help, but it was locked. I banged on it and banged on it, but no one came."

I sat him up and checked him for injuries, allowing him to pause and tell me the story at his own pace. "By that time, the thing was inside the room. I turned around and it had Lupita by the neck. She was struggling and struggling, but she couldn't get loose. Elena was screaming and screaming— the thing broke her mom's neck. It was so loud I could hear the crack, even with Elena screaming at the top of her lungs.

Then he dropped her and reached for Elena, so—I rushed at it to try to save her. That's all I remember."

He hung his head and started to cry. "It took her, didn't it? I told you! I told you something bad was gonna happen, but you didn't listen! Now Elena's gone and that thing killed her mom, and it's your fault!" He screamed the last bit at me, and turned away.

I sighed. "Look, kid, I had no idea something like this would happen. Heck, I saw it take off with her, and I still can barely believe what I saw. The thing is, we can't stay here. Whatever it is that took Elena is long gone, and if we stay here it's going to come back for us too. Best that we just leave and put this behind us before we end up dead as well."

He turned toward me, and I didn't need lights to see the look of accusation on his face. "You're a coward. You're a coward, and I'm sorry I ever agreed to help you!"

Before responding, I paused and took a deep breath. "Maybe so, kid, but I'm a living coward. And I'll be honest, I don't like this whole deal any more than you do. But I plan to have my ass on the road and long gone before that thing comes back. Now, you can stay here or you can come with me; it's up to you. But I'm out of here regardless of your decision or how you feel about me."

Right about then, the sound of the window creaking open interrupted our argument. We both turned to look, and I saw the very thing that had killed Lupita and taken Elena just moments before, crawling through the window Gollum-style to finish what it had started. The kid froze like a spotlighted deer, and all I could think was that I was hella glad I had some firepower with me, because this thing looked like the grim reaper itself. Without a second to spare, I pushed Rayden behind me and reached for my Glock, hoping like hell that 200 grain hollow points would be enough to take this thing down.

11

CRY

WHATEVER IT WAS, it was definitely not human, although it had humanoid characteristics. It moved like a cross between a spider and a snake, with rapid skittering movements that were disconcertingly sinuous and bug-like all at once. Strangely, it wore fatigues, combat boots, and a rain poncho with the hood pulled up. I couldn't see a face, but I guessed it was going to be ugly by the way it moved.

"Screw me blue and call me Willy Wonka," I muttered as I pulled my Glock and drew a bead on the thing.

As I fired, I took a lesson from my previous experiences with the deaders and immediately started going for head-shots. Now, a lot of people think that just because you're an Army Ranger and you were in the "Special Forces" you can shoot the balls off a gnat at 300 yards with just about any firearm. And, they're wrong. Most of the guys I knew in the Regiment never touched a pistol except for recreation, although almost every one of them could place a nice tight grouping in the ten ring at 300 yards with an M4. And the snipers? Forget it. Those guys are trained to be 100 percent successful in taking out a target at over 800 yards in two shots or less.

But again, when it came to being a serious shooter with a sidearm, most Rangers weren't. Personally, my handgunning skills were limited to growing up plinking on the ranch, taking a few combat shooting courses before and after my time in the service, and also spending not an inconsiderable amount of time on the range with a handgun. So, I was definitely no slouch, but I was no freaking Doc Holiday, that's for sure, and this thing took full advantage of my lack of accuracy to keep me from planting one in its noggin. As soon as I fired the first shot, it started pulling an Agent Smith on me, displaying contortions with its spine and neck that no human ever could... and especially not at that speed.

I used one arm to keep the kid behind me and angled away from it as it stalked us, tossing a desk over and kicking a cot in its way as it came at us. As I'd hoped, it decided to come around the mess rather than over it, and that's when I stitched it right up the torso with three well-placed shots, one right after another. It was a technique I'd learned from a homicide cop I'd trained with, using the recoil of the weapon to hit multiple torso targets, "stitching" an assailant right up the centerline.

As it so happened, my first shot was off-center and I caught it in the right hip. I saw it falter as it took another step, so I fired the remainder of the magazine into its torso. It screamed bloody murder with a wail that would have given a banshee a run for her money. Suddenly, it snatched up Lupita's corpse and bolted for the window almost faster than my eyes could track. I figured I must have hurt it, but the fact that it was still moving fast despite any injuries it might have sustained gave me pause. Before I could even drop the empty mag and reload, it went out the window. I rushed over to see which way it was headed, and thought I saw a shadow going the same direction it had just a few minutes prior.

I turned to the kid and checked him over to make sure he was alright. He shrugged me off and pouted himself over to a nearby cot. "That thing was coming back for me," he said, and his voice trembled in fear as he spoke.

It was really the first time I'd seen the kid rattled since I met him. Oh, he'd been a little riled back at the tanker, but this was pure, unadulterated fear he experienced. I knew, because I'd experienced it myself the first time my unit had seen combat. Fact was I had nearly shit myself the first time I saw the elephant, and I'm not ashamed to admit it.

His face was illuminated by the fluorescent light streaming in from the hallway, and I could see the look of fear and desperation on his face as he pleaded with me. "I couldn't even help her, and she's just a little kid. You have to go after her, Sully. You have to!"

It only took me a moment to decide. After seeing that thing, I knew I just couldn't stand around and let a child be terrorized and killed by something like that. I also realized that if I didn't go after Elena, it would haunt me until the day I died.

I nodded, and I could see the kid's posture relax a little.

"Alright, but if I'm going to follow it we need to get a move on. For one, those soldiers are going to be up here soon to see what all the commotion was, although I figure they already have a clue as to what might have happened. Also, I'm going to need to get you someplace safer than this before daylight, because there's no way I'm leaving you with these people."

"You think they set us up?"

"Yeah, kid, I do. I don't know why, but if you put two and two together it's the only thing that makes sense." I counted off on my fingers as I broke it down. "One: the people disappearing that Bibi told us about. Two: the fact that they separated us from the rest of the people staying here. None of the locals were placed in this room with us. In fact, we're about as far from the rest of the refugees as can be. Three: all that crazy talk Lupita was spouting. And four: the fact that they locked us in. Look, we'll talk about it more once we get you someplace safe, but we're not staying in this loony bin another minute. Let's go."

The kid got up to follow me, and then he stopped suddenly. "What if that thing is waiting for us?"

"It's not. I think I hurt it—and besides, it probably figures we'll sit tight and hunker down. The last thing it's expecting is to be hunted, which is probably going to make it hella easy to track." I paused. "Look, I know I was being selfish, but I'm going to get her back."

He didn't say a word after that, the whole way back to the truck.

———

JUST TO BE SAFE, we broke into a garage apartment across the street from where I'd parked the truck. Lots of homes in Fredericksburg had them, as bed and breakfasts were a major part of the economy in these parts. Sure enough, this one was set up more like a hotel room than an apartment, with a combination bedroom and living area just as we walked in, a bath off to the side, a small kitchenette with a sink, a dorm fridge, and a microwave. I got the kid settled in and made sure he had food and water in case I didn't come back that night. I sure as hell didn't want him out sneaking around, even to go to the truck across the street. We had no idea what was stalking the night out there, and I had no intentions of him getting taken by the boogie man.

After that I waited until it was getting light, then snuck back over to the high school to start tracking that thing. I had to be extra careful; I didn't want the guards or sheriff's deputies to see me, and I preferred them simply assuming we had all been taken in the night by our mysterious and creepy visitor. I had a feeling they wouldn't be looking for me, but after I picked up the trail I didn't take any chances, keeping a low profile as I followed the signs the creature left to where it was headed.

Picking up the trail wasn't all that difficult; it left quite an indentation in the ground when it landed. I guessed that 200-some-odd pounds of monster and corpse would do that upon jumping a two stories to the ground. I also spotted some blood spatters, not much but enough to track by. It was tacky, dark, and looked older than it should have been. There was definitely not as much as I would have expected, considering how many times I'd hit it. That told me what all the other information I'd gathered thus far had been pointing to; this thing, whatever it was, was something other than human.

I tried to psyche myself up, knowing that I needed to be all business from here on out. *No shit it's not human, Sully. It's about time you woke up and faced the fact that your world has entered the twilight zone. Now, quit being a pussy and to get to work.*

Once I had my head right I followed the trail further into town, dodging a roving patrol along the way. The thing had apparently been moving at the same speed the entire time, and it either wasn't aware it was leaving a trail, or it didn't care. Despite the urban environment I was able to track it based on the signs it left. Well, that and the occasional drops of blood I found every ten paces or so. After a while, I realized that it moved in a straight line toward the Gillespie County Airport. As I recalled, there wasn't much out that way—just a few hangars, a diner that catered to the private pilots who flew in and out of there, and a hotel.

I was betting that it was using one of the hangars or the hotel to hole up in, and if I had to guess it would be one of the hangars. Although Fredericksburg was just 60 miles or so from Austin as the crow flies, most airplanes would've survived the overpressure, which normally would crumple small aircraft within 20 miles or so of an atomic detonation. However, I bet that the sensitive electronics in many of the small craft that were stored there would've been fried by the EMP, and I also guessed that anyone who tried to exfil through here would be like sitting ducks to this thing. Strategically, if I were a top-tier predator looking for easy human prey and little to no human intervention, it's where I would've set up in a crisis like this.

As I neared the airport, the foliage became thicker and the thing was easier to track. Although I had a pretty clear idea of where it was headed, I continued to track it without deviating from the trail it had left. This took me through a few empty fields as well as the fairgrounds, which thankfully hadn't been mowed in a while, making my job as simple as keeping an eye out for an ambush and walking in a straight line to the hangar dead ahead.

Once I got to the airfield, I snuck around the back of the closest hangar making as little noise as possible. As far as I was concerned, my best chance at killing this thing was surprise. Even injured, I'd seen it move faster than any human, and I doubted that I'd be a match for it in close quarters. Well, maybe if I had a *katana*, but I was shit out of those at the moment. Funny how random weapons never show up at opportune times in real life like they do in video games and horror movies.

Once I'd found the side entrance, I stopped to do a quick gear and ammo check. A press check of the M4 told me I had one in the chamber, and I'd swapped out for a full mag right before I left Rayden. I had my Bowie knife, my combat folder, my Glock and my Kahr. All things considered, I was pretty well set on the armament front. I still would have gladly traded at least one of the sidearms for a tactical *katana*, or a nice traditional *shinken* type made for cutting through straw mats and people like butter. But, you play with the hand you're dealt.

After my equipment check I kept moving and found the side door in short order. I noticed more of that dark and not-quite-human looking blood on the door handle, and knew I'd definitely tracked this thing to its lair. The door was solid steel with no window, and chances were good the beast would see the light from the door if it was anywhere near the entrance when I cracked it open. I decided to take my chances, turning the knob ever so slowly until I felt it give. I swung open the door and moved in quickly, scanning and sweeping the area with the rifle in one hand, shutting the door behind me as quietly as possible.

As soon as I entered and my heart stopped beating through my chest, I heard the kid crying at the back of the hangar. It looked like there were some administrative offices or maintenance areas in the back, built out of metal studs and drywall with drop ceilings and little else to muffle external noise. I would use that to my advantage.

I moved toward the back, navigating my way past a nice Cessna and two WWII-era relics that had been fully restored. I paused beside the Cessna and listened for any movement, then moved forward, scanning left to right. I also kept an eye on the rafters overhead, as the threat of an ambush from above seemed to be a real possibility. Nothing. Finally I approached the office area in the back and pinned myself up against the wall, slowing my breathing and listening for any sound or lack of sound that might have indicated I'd been noticed.

As I listened, I could hear a voice underneath the kid's sobs. It was as rough and dry as a *caliche* pit in summer, and hearing it made my skin crawl all over.

"Now, now, little bird, you mustn't cry. It'll all be over soon. Yes, soon."

I took that as a signal that it was feeding time at the monster zoo, so I hurried down the hall to the doorway where the noise was coming from. The door had been left ajar, and although the lights were off I could see a dark figure looming at the back corner across from my vantage point, as well as the kid's shoe and ankle.

I sighted in on the thing's back and opened fire, aiming high for fear of a round over-penetrating and hitting the kid.

The staccato sound of the M4 rattled off the walls within the enclosed space, and 5.56 shells spat out of my rifle like rain, hitting the floor with sharp little pings as they fell. I connected with the first two shots, one near the spine and another at the shoulder, then the next six or seven missed as the thing zig-zagged off to the side like nothing I'd ever seen. I tracked it around the room as it moved, finally getting wise and leading it to plant two more hits, one in the torso and the other in its head, or at least in its hood. I couldn't tell if I'd made a headshot or not, but as I backed out of the room to draw it away from the child it visibly slowed, if not to human speed, then just enough to hopefully give me a fighting chance.

I emptied the mag at it as it followed me out of the room and down the short hall to the hangar. When the bolt locked open on an empty chamber, I dropped the mag and slapped another one in, depressing the bolt catch and racking a fresh round. I pulled the trigger and was rewarded with dull "click," which told me I had a failure-to-feed malfunction. I'd cleared these sorts of weapon malfunctions dozens of times in training and in combat, yet I had little time to do so before the thing was on top of me. Out of options, I stabbed the barrel at its face, aiming for the eye socket, a nasty trick that was made nastier by the fact that I had a wicked striking bezel on the end of my flash hider.

Of course, the thing moved its head out of the way like Pacquiao, bobbing and weaving around the muzzle of my rifle. Even so, the muzzle snagged on its hood, pulling it back to reveal what I was dealing with. The thing looked to have been human at some point, as I could recognize the resemblance, but his facial skin was stretched and drawn, with a color and texture that reminded me of a rhino or an elephant. The eyes were dark yellow around the irises, which were almost non-existent as the pupils were two black nickels in a sea of yellow sclera. I could see where a round had hit it in the face, as a perfect little hole punched into its face just to the right of its nostrils. A small bead of blood oozed out, but revealed no significant blood loss. Its hair was falling out in clumps, and what once looked to have been a neatly coiffed shock of bright red hair was now just ragged patches of stubble and mange.

I noted all these details in an instant, right before it shied away to cover its eyes and draw its hood back up. I realized then that the thing's eyes were adapted for the dark, and that it must've lacked the ability to contract its pupils sufficiently to shield them from daytime light.

Gotcha, I thought as I backpedaled and reached for the light switch I'd noticed on the way in. As soon as I hit the lights, it screeched like it had back at the school and bounded off down the hall to the room where it had left the kid.

"Shit!" I hollered as I dropped my rifle and ran after it, drawing the Glock and firing as it flowed through the dark doorway. I hit the doorway and jagged right, only to see the thing fly up through the ceiling tiles as I flicked the lights on. Thankfully, the kid was still whimpering in the corner. Secure in the knowledge that it wouldn't be following us outside, I grabbed her and headed toward a door I'd seen at the end of the hall, hitting the release bar at a run and dumping us both on the ground outside.

Elena clung to me and cried, whimpering in Spanish and begging me to take her to her mommy. I didn't have time to be heartbroken, and ran with her about 30 yards away from the building to a line of vehicles in the parking lot. I set her down on the hood of a vintage Ford pickup and raised her head gently so I could make eye contact.

"Tengo que ir a matar el cucuy. Espera aquí. Voy a volver en un momento." *I have to go kill the monster. Stay here. I'll be back for you in a moment.*

She cried and shook her head no, clinging to me for all she was worth. But I knew I had hurt that thing, and I felt that if I didn't finish the job it would just kill again... tonight, and the next night, and the next. I spent several more minutes calming her down, and finally was able to convince her to release me so I could go back and end it for good. After she'd settled down enough to let me go, I assured her that I'd come back for her and told her to stay put, but to head back to the high school if I didn't come back out soon. Then I headed back inside the hangar, determined to kill that thing or die trying.

12

CHARGING

I RELOADED and entered the building from the side entrance again, both in an attempt to avoid an ambush from overhead and also so I'd be entering on familiar ground. The way that thing shot up through the ceiling tiles, I had no doubts that it would be waiting high above me in an ambush position. So I opted to enter the building via the hangar area, where I'd at least have a clear 360 view of my surroundings.

I stopped immediately after entering the hangar, pausing under the wing of the Cessna as I listened for any signs of movement. Momentarily, I was greeted by the same gravelly voice I'd heard earlier.

"Come back to finish me off, eh? I doubted anyone around here would have the balls to go against the commander, but obviously you're not from around here, are you?" His voice again grated on my nerves like a splinter under every fingernail. There was just something otherworldly and entirely unsettling about it that made my skin crawl.

I paused to process what he'd said before I carefully framed my answer. "I figured you were somehow working with the local authorities, but I'm curious how that came to be. Did you threaten them with violence?"

It laughed, a harsh sound that carried both screeching high notes and a low solid rumble. It was probably the most inhuman and frightening sound I'd ever heard in my life. "No, little man. That was not necessary."

I decided to keep it talking so I could pinpoint its location, and angled my voice toward the back of the hangar to keep it from knowing I was stalking it. "Okay, then tell me why they don't come out here with some major firepower and blow your ass back to the hell you came from? You and I both know they have the ordinance."

There was a pregnant and rather unsettling stretch of silence before it replied. "Humans. You are all so predictable. I am—was—the commander's son, serving in his unit as a subordinate. As it happens, he is loath to kill his only son. A situation that I find to be—ironic."

Well, that explained a helluva lot. I kept pressing for info. "Still, what I don't get is how you convinced him and the deputies to let you just take people right out from under their noses. Obviously, someone is missing these people and asking questions." As I spoke, I continued to try to pin its location down, but couldn't seem to get a lock on it. I decided to go with Plan B and started working my way to the front of the hangar.

"We simply made a deal. I keep the dead away from their little sanctuary, and they provide me with the castaways from their group. Outsiders, the homeless, and those from foreign lands. No one notices these people, and no one cares that they're gone."

I allowed myself a chuckle. "Well, that's where you're wrong, asshole. People do care. How do you think I was tipped off to all this shit? Well, besides you killing and kidnapping people. I got news for you, there are people back at that high school who are asking questions, and I have a feeling that your *dad* is going to have a hard time keeping a lid on it. Just wait until the government gets a grip on this situation, because I can guarantee you that everyone involved is going down."

I heard it make a noise, and at first I thought it was choking on a bone or coughing up a hairball. Eventually I realized that it was laughing at my comment about the government. Not with the Vincent Price from hell laugh I'd heard a minute ago... this time it was truly and genuinely amused by what I'd just said.

After a minute, the laughter died down and it spoke. "The government? You think that the government is going to swoop in and save you? You have no idea how bad things are for your species right now, or what's to come. You are no longer the apex predator on this planet, and as of a few days ago your species has become meat for my kind. You are now nothing more than cattle, purposely left alive so we can slaughter you at our leisure."

That sort of threw me for a loop. "Wait a minute—you mean there are more like you?"

"Yes, and we are a legion." It paused, and I thought I'd

heard it wheeze, which meant it either had a cold or I'd hurt it badly earlier. I banked on the latter. "But, you'll never see them—at least, not in this life." And that's when I knew the thing was coming for me. I felt more than heard it drop to the hangar floor and sprint toward me.

I hit the button that opened the hangar door.

The sudden burst of sunlight halted the thing in its tracks. As it slid to a stop and covered its face, I quickly drew a bead and started taking precision shots, aiming for its joints as I walked forward. Left knee. Right knee. Elbow. Shoulder. Within seconds the accumulated effects of each hit took their toll, and it was a quivering, mewling mass on the floor. I sauntered up and methodically reloaded as it started crawling toward the back of the hangar. Thanking the Man above for this bright, sunny Texas day, I started putting rounds in its head, one after another until it finally stopped moving.

———

AFTER THE SOUND of gunfire stopped ringing in my ears, I found that I desperately wanted to get the hell out of there, to just take Elena and Rayden back to the ranch and hole up there until Kingdom come. But, I had two things weighing on my mind at the moment: one being my parents, and two being the fact that I was hella curious to see what this thing was all about.

So I pulled it out onto the tarmac and studied it thoroughly with the hunter's eye for detail that my grandfather had instilled in me years before. I removed its clothing, piece by piece. Sure enough, it was still wearing dog tags that identified it as Robert L. Hillis, blood type AB negative, Catholic. *Interesting.*

I examined the body with a coroner's care, taking note of every detail. I assumed that in the future I might come across one of these things again, so I wasn't taking any chances. I started with the head and mouth, noticing the changes in the eyes, a shriveling of the cartilage in the nose and ears, and the loss of hair. Pulling back the lips, I saw that several of its teeth were loose. Not wanting to risk any chance of infection, I pulled out my multi-tool and used the pliers to pull one out. Underneath, I could see the point of a sharp, almost shark-like tooth poking its way up through the gum line to replace it.

Moving down the body, the same changes in skin color and texture were noticeable all over. I noted that the body was hairless, although the thing's genitalia were intact. What was incredibly frightening was that it'd been hit more times than I'd thought, maybe with a few dozen rounds. Despite all that damage, until I'd started taking the strategic approach to round placement it had still been able to function. That told me it didn't necessarily rely on internal organs to keep its motor functions going; in other words, it didn't experience shock like a human would. Scary, but fascinating.

I continued my examination by moving to the limbs, and saw that the fingernails and toenails were also falling out, being replaced with what looked like thicker and more claw-like nails. The bones in the hands and the feet also appeared to be elongating, although that could have just been a congenital defect. Overall, though, it was apparent that this thing had once been human, but it had been in the process of morphing into something much more hideous and dangerous.

I filed the info away for future reference, then went back to check on Elena. She sat stock still on the hood of the truck, just where I'd left her. Once I knew she was fine, I started rummaging around in the hangar for more clues regarding the nature of this thing. In my search, I found a room stacked up with rotting corpses, all of which had been savaged at the throat and drained of blood.

Realization dawned on me like a bolt of lightning. *Holy shit, that thing was an honest-to-goodness vampire. We're not in Kansas anymore, Toto.*

After no small amount of thought, I settled on what I had to do. I wrapped it up in a tarp and threw it in the back of the old pickup. It only took a few minutes to figure out how to hotwire the old girl, and she started up like a dream. I got Elena buckled in and headed back to where I'd left Rayden, so I could drop her off with him while I took care of business. He was happy to see her alive and well, but he was also uncharacteristically quiet. He was probably in shock, but I could do nothing about it at the moment. Once I made sure they were settled in, I headed over to the high school.

———

I PULLED RIGHT UP to the back loading docks, because I knew that was probably where they brought in supplies that they'd scrounged from around the area. I left my rifle in the truck behind the seat and moved my sidearm around to the small of my back, concealing it under the flannel shirt I was wearing. I decided to act like I belonged here, hoping that I'd be able to bluff my way through. Grabbing the covered body of Hillis' son from the back of the truck, I slung it over my shoulder and marched right up to the loading dock doors.

A soldier stopped me at the door. "Whoa, where do you think you're going?"

I pointed at the wrapped up corpse on my back. "Deputy Carson said y'all needed meat. I used to be a guide at the Y.O. Ranch, so he asked me to go out and hunt some deer from one of the local ranches. I'm delivering a doe I shot this morning."

"First I heard of it, but alright. Just make sure you don't scare anyone when you take that thing into the mess hall."

I nodded. "Oh, I wouldn't dream of it."

Once inside I made a beeline to the cafeteria, where I knew everyone would be gathered in preparation for midday chow. I marched right up to the center of the room, hopped up on a table, and dumped the body in the middle, unfurling it from the tarp for all the world to see. That pretty much got everyone's attention, and soon people started crowding around and murmuring amongst themselves.

"What is that thing?"

"Is it one of those infected?"

"Looks like a monster—not even human."

And so on. Their reactions varied, but I wasn't interested in sparking speculation. Soldiers would come to break this up soon, so I had to act fast to get the word out about what Hillis had been doing.

I cleared my throat, and spoke up in my best command voice. "Folks, what you see before you is a different kind of creature from the infected you're already familiar with. I tracked this one to the airport, right after it came into the room I'd been assigned here and attacked the people who were sleeping there. Unlike the infected, these things are intelligent and capable of speech, and this one told me he'd made a deal with Captain Hillis."

Someone shouted from the crowd. "To do what?"

"To hunt and kill you—or, more specifically, to kill those of you who wouldn't be missed. That's where the missing people have gone. Before I killed it, this thing told me that it had worked out a deal with the commander to help keep the infected away from this compound, in exchange for human lives. A few here, a few there, and always people who wouldn't be missed. Immigrants and those who had no family with them."

At that, the crowd burst into an uproar, and I could see that the soldiers in the cafeteria had no idea what to do. One of them was on his comms, but in the commotion all I could tell was that he talked a hundred miles a minute. A few others chattered amongst themselves, probably conferring about what I'd just revealed. I was hoping their civilian soldier status would work in my favor, that this would spark a combined revolt between the people and the close-knit group of soldiers who must've been helping Hillis to keep up his charade. Considering the timeline, it couldn't have been going on for long, so I suspected only a few soldiers and cops knew the full story.

Once the crowd worked into a frenzy, I knew it was high time to make myself scarce. I'd done my good deed for the day and then some, and I was ready to get back on the road. The fact that my parents were facing this mess alone weighed on me heavily, but unfortunately now I had two extra souls to look after. I needed to think things through before I headed out, because there was no way I was getting back on the road with that little girl in tow. Rayden was one thing; he could more or less fend for himself. But Elena would just slow us down, and I wasn't about to get her killed by taking her on the road with us.

I made a snap decision and started looking for Bibi as I worked my way out of the crowd. I finally spotted her sitting off to the side, sipping a cup of coffee and observing the ruckus. I moved over to her as quickly as possible without mowing anyone over.

"Well, you sure stirred things up here, didn't you?" she said as I walked up to her table. "I knew that Hillis was up to no good, but I never expected something like this. You look like hell."

"If you knew the night I just had, you'd understand. Look Bibi, I don't have much time. Before long Hillis is going to have people looking for me, and I need to get out of town before he does. Only problem is, I have a kid with me who needs looking after."

She nodded sagely. "That boy who was with you?"

I shook my head. "Nope, a little girl who was bunked with us last night. That thing over there killed her mom." I tilted my head toward the bloodsucker, hesitating to say what I thought it was out loud. "Think you can help out?"

She stood up and pulled her jacket around her. "I'm too old to be looking after a young child, but I'm sure I can find someone to take care of her. Question is, is this the safest place for her to be right now?"

"Well, I've seen what it's like outside these fences, and I'd have to say it is. Not that I trust Hillis to be in charge here—but I don't think he will be for long."

She glanced over at the people crowding around the corporal's corpse and gave me a look of disgust. They were now in the process of being dispersed by some soldiers, but the crowd wasn't having it. I knew that pretty soon they'd be crying out for blood.

I motioned for her to follow. "Come on, I have a truck parked around back. Also got a safe place for you and the kid to stay until things blow over. You can come back here once the smoke has settled."

She barked a short laugh and rolled her eyes at me. "The hell I will! If you get me out of here, there's no way I'm coming back. Just promise me you'll pass through to check on us on your way back from getting your folks."

I took that to mean that she was going to look after Elena after all, but I didn't bother to ask for clarification. By the time we were leaving the building more soldiers were headed in that direction. They were obviously preoccupied with the disturbance I'd caused, so they ignored us as we headed down the halls toward the loading docks.

A few minutes later we were in the truck, headed back to

the house where I'd left Rayden and Elena. As I drove past the front of the high school, we heard shots fired. I could only hope that they were for Hillis and those who helped him, and not for the innocent people who had looked to the military for help in a crisis. Far be it from me to take on an entire battalion of soldiers, though; I'd done my part, now it was up to them.

[13]

SUFFOCATING

It didn't take long for Bibi to gain Elena's trust. I figured the kid would take to her, since she put off a serious grandma vibe of the kind kids can't resist. I got Bibi settled in at the little cottage, then spent about half an hour raiding nearby homes for food and supplies to see them through until things calmed down. I promised to check back in on them in a few days on my way back from Austin, and left Bibi my beloved Kahr .45 and a box of ammo, along with my spare magazines. She accepted them without comment.

Rayden seemed to have a hard time leaving Elena behind. He spent a few moments with her, and I noticed that she'd somehow ended up with a rag doll in the time since I'd left them earlier that day. The kid had a soft touch, that was for sure. Resourceful, too. I thought about it as we loaded up, and finally took him off to the side away from Elena and Bibi to talk.

"Look, kid, I know you're shook up about what happened

last night. I also think you can help Elena and Bibi a helluva lot more than you can help me. That's why I think it's best if you stay here with them until I get back."

He chewed his lip and looked at the ground. "You mean *if* you make it back."

I tilted my head and nodded. "You know as well as I do how hairy things are out there. No need to lie; I'd say there's a fifty-fifty chance I won't make it back. All the more reason for you to stay here. Besides, you got skills and you're a survivor. You can do a lot of good by staying behind and looking after Bibi and Elena."

He turned to face me and looked me in the eye, extending his hand. "I won't let you down."

I shook his hand. "I know you won't, kid. You've proven yourself already, believe me. I've served with guys who didn't have the guts you've shown. Now, just keep your head down, stay hidden for a few days until I get back, and if I don't make it back in three days you'll know you're on your own. At that point, I suggest that you see if things have settled down at the high school, because staying with a large group is going to be your best bet."

He nodded. "Bring me back some Ding Dongs and a Mountain Dew."

"You got it." I slapped him on the back and went to say goodbye to Bibi and Elena.

Once it looked like the roads were clear, I drove a few blocks over to head out one of the gates the soldiers had set up when they cordoned off the area. There were no guards present, which I took as a sign that everyone had been called back to the high school. There'd been sporadic gunfire coming from that direction since Bibi and I split, and I hoped things would settle down before the violence got too severe.

The gate was padlocked, so I cut the lock with my bolt cutters and drove through. Then I secured the gate again with some baling wire I had in the back of the truck. Once I had the gate secured, I took the long way around town until I got back to the highway. Checking my map, I decided I'd take 183 north at Johnsonville, then I'd take 1431 at Marble Falls. That'd take me almost right to my parent's house, or damned close to it. I hit 290 and headed out at a good clip, utilizing the shoulder to get around stalled cars and wrecks.

Once I got closer to Johnson City, I started to see more stalled cars and a lot more deaders. In more than one instance I had to do some fancy driving to avoid clusters of them milling about in the road. I decided to stick to the back streets at Johnson City, to avoid being stopped by the authorities. I needn't have worried. The town was dead, in the most literal sense, from what I could tell. I saw lots of broken windows and smashed doors as I drove through, along with a large number of corpses, moving and not.

As I was driving through the north side of town, I saw a sheriff's vehicle pulled over on the side of the road. The driver's side door was open, and I slowed down to see what had happened. Inside, an officer slumped over the steering wheel, his brains splattered all over the inside of the car. Another suicide. I looked around to make sure no deaders were close by, then I put the truck in neutral, set the parking brake, and jumped out. A search of the car yielded a Glock

9mm, a few spare mags, a Remington model 870 shotgun with a box of ammo, and an AR-15. I said a silent prayer for the officer and his family as I drove away.

————

THE REST of the afternoon proceeded without incident. I blew through Round Mountain, and other than avoiding a large pile-up at the intersection of 71 and 281, the road was more or less clear once I left Johnson City. The only thing that really worried me was crossing the Colorado River in Marble Falls. As I recalled, that bridge had two lanes in either direction, so all it would take was a bad accident or some troublemakers to keep me from crossing.

Sure enough, my fears were well founded. As I drove up to the bridge I could see that it was clogged with stalled cars in both directions. I backed up and headed for the ford below the dam. I'd gone fishing there once with some friends, and with any luck the dam wouldn't be running and the water would be low enough to cross.

I drove down old Wirtz Dam Road with my hopes high. Unfortunately, as I neared the dam it became apparent that I was shit out of luck. Someone in charge must've had the foresight to open the floodgates before the power went completely out, so there was no way I was making it through that crossing. In a few days, maybe, but at the moment the water was at least two feet above the road and flowing fast. No way I could risk it.

I slammed my hands on the steering wheel and weighed

my options. I could head back to 71 and take it into southwest Austin, but that would mean I'd have to drive through some of the most populated areas of the city to get to my folks' house. I didn't even want to think about the carnage created by the blast, never mind all the deaders that would be milling around. Definitely a last resort.

I could also head east on 71 and then cut over to Kingsland, but I'd probably be facing a similar situation. The bridge there was a narrow two-lane, and it might be blocked as well. That would cost me precious time, but at least if that didn't work out I could cut north and take 29 instead. Not my ideal route, but it would do. I U-turned and headed back down the road.

———

IT WAS nightfall before I reached the outskirts of Austin, which in reality were smaller towns, bedroom communities for people who'd worked in the city proper. Cedar Park, Leander, and Round Rock had all started out as sleepy little towns before the boom hit Austin and the city's population exploded. Folks native to Austin would tell you that all the growth had ruined the city. *There's not much to complain about at the moment,* I thought, *nor people left to complain.* I started to get pissed. Before I got too worked up, though, I put those thoughts out of my mind and started focusing on my game plan.

My parents lived in an upscale neighborhood on the edge of town, between Round Rock and Cedar Park. I could cut south from 29 and take the Parmer Lane extension almost to my parent's front door. The only question was how bad things were in their general vicinity. I could only hope that they'd been able to hunker down and wait it out. That's if they were still alive.

It took me some time to make it to their neighborhood, as the roads continued to be clogged up with stalled cars, more wrecks, and the living dead. I was shocked at how many shamblers I saw, and decided that the commander hadn't lied to me about the infection rate. I spent a lot of time driving on the shoulder to get around large groups of deaders and motor vehicle pile-ups, and saw a lot of things I wished I hadn't seen. It was after midnight before I made it to my parent's place. As I pulled up to their house, things didn't look promising.

There were no lights on in the neighborhood, so I parked the truck so that its headlights would illuminate the front of the house. I grabbed my M4 and an extra tactical flashlight, turned the truck off and locked it, then I headed to the front of the house. I could hear and see deaders converging on my position from around the area, so I knew I didn't have a lot of time. I sprinted up the front walk to the door, noting that it had been kicked in.

I decided on speed over stealth, and began calling out for my parents as I entered the home, clearing the entry and living room on the way. "Mom! Dad! Anyone here! Answer me if you can hear me!" Hearing no answer, I paused to put the door back in place and barricaded it with some furniture to prevent any deaders from surprising me on the way back out.

After moving the couch and loveseat against the door, I heard something fall over in the kitchen, followed by shuffling footsteps from that direction. I prayed that it wouldn't be one of my parents, and headed that way using the flashlight on my rifle to light my path. I paused against the wall just outside the kitchen and waited as the footsteps got closer. I heard a low moan, and then a figure shuffled around the corner. The light blinded it temporarily, and it shielded its face as it continued to shuffle toward me.

It was, or had been, Mr. Keller, the neighbor from across the street. Not wanting to draw more attention than I already had, I pulled out my combat Bowie and buried it to the hilt in the top of his head. He almost pulled me down as he collapsed, so I let go of the blade to let him fall. After retrieving my knife and cleaning it on his shirt, I sheathed it and continued clearing the first floor. I noticed signs that someone had packed in a hurry, but I didn't see any indication of a struggle—nor did I see my parents... dead or alive.

I headed upstairs to find more rooms devoid of life. Although I found indications that they'd packed and left in a rush, there was nothing to tell me where they had went or where to find them. Dejected, I sat down on my parents' bed wondering what my next move should be.

Think, Aidan, think! Mom and Dad wouldn't leave without letting you know where they went. So, how would they let you know where they were going?

I pondered it for a moment, until my thoughts were interrupted by something banging on the front door. It wouldn't hold for long, so I needed to complete my search and escape pronto. I racked my brain for ideas, and then it dawned on me. When I was just a kid, sometimes my mom would leave a note for me when I got home from school. She had been working as a nurse back then, and often had to work shifts that prevented her from being home when I got off the school bus.

She'd always hated leaving notes out in the open, saying that if someone broke in it would tell them that no one was home. Never mind that once someone broke in the house it wouldn't have mattered; there was no arguing with Mom logic. To prevent burglars who broke in from knowing they were alone, she'd always leave any notes for me in the cookie jar.

I sprinted downstairs and looked on top of the fridge; sure enough, I saw the same ceramic rooster cookie jar we'd had as a kid. I'd thought the thing had been broken or lost decades before, but obviously Mom had put it up, probably to give to me as a wedding gift or something. I pulled it down and set it on the table, pulling off the lid to find a note scribbled on legal paper inside.

Aidan,

We couldn't wait any longer since things have gotten really bad over the last few days. Your father borrowed Mr. Keller's motor home; I guess he won't be needing it anymore and it was the only thing around here that your dad could find that still runs. Your dad left you a map with

the route he plans to take to get us out to the ranch. Look
under the cookie jar for it. We love you, mijo.

- Mom

P.S. - Dad says to tell you it's a 1989 Winnebago
Chieftain. Gold and white with blue and gold stripes.

I reached on top of the refrigerator and found the map
she'd mentioned. Unfolding it, I saw that he planned to take
1431 to 281, a route almost identical to the one I'd taken to
get here. Since I didn't see recall seeing a motorhome that fit
that description along the way, I figured they'd gotten
stranded or held up somewhere between here and Marble
Falls. The only way to find them would be to trace their route
and hope I could catch up with them before they ran into
trouble.

By that time, the pounding on the front door was getting
more frenzied; it sounded like the deaders were almost inside.
Amidst a chorus of moans and groans, I stuck the map and
note in my pocket, grabbed my rifle, and headed for the back
door. Then, as an afterthought, I went back and tucked the
cookie jar under my arm before taking off at a jog.

[14]

SUCCESS

As I EXITED the backyard and cleared the corner of the house, I noted that most of the deaders had gathered around the front door. I assumed that the noise I'd made when I barricaded the door had been enough to attract a few, and the noise they'd made in turn had drawn in the rest. I jogged up to the truck as silently as I could, opening and shutting the cab door before they even noticed my presence. From what I could tell, their eyesight was shit but their hearing was excellent, and as soon as I started the truck they began shuffling my way.

I had the truck in gear and was backing up long before they got close to the truck, but in my haste to get out of there I backed over a few of them. Figured I was doing them a favor, and thankfully the heavy duty bumper I had on the back of the truck made short work of them. Sadly though, I spun the tires on one of the corpses as I was taking off and ended up with a slow one hanging onto the driver's side mirror as I drove away.

That son of a gun was strong, and held on with one arm while the other beat on the glass for all he was worth, leaving blood and pus on the window with each glancing blow. I considered drawing my sidearm and shooting him. But I couldn't see how I was going to roll the window down while swerving to avoid the numerous shamblers that roamed the streets, all while firing a pistol at a target that was determined to climb into the cab with me. Finally, I drove close to a parked car and knocked him off, but not before he bent up my side view mirror mount. I was starting to realize that zombies were hell on automobiles, and made a mental note to keep an eye out for another Hilux that I could use for parts once I got back home.

But, first things first: I had to figure out where Mom and Dad were. I tried the cell that I'd found out in the woods, but there was zero cell service in the area. EMP had probably fried the towers, and considering that it was pitch black all over the area it probably burned out the grid too. I kept my high beams on and drove a lot slower that I might have liked, avoiding random collisions with shamblers more than once as I drove out of town.

By the time I got to 1431 and 183, it was time to gas up the beast. Thankfully, there was no shortage of stalled cars around; I just had to find one that was isolated enough so I didn't have to fear getting bum-rushed by deaders. I pulled around the back of a grocery store, figuring I'd only have two directions to watch as I filled my gas cans; sure enough, there was a Chevy Tahoe parked behind the building.

As I pulled up, I inched forward with my brights directed at the cab, but saw no movement inside. I grabbed the M4, kept the truck running with the parking brake set, and went around back to grab the gas cans and siphon hose. I dumped the contents of the cans in my tank, and then inched over to the Tahoe to see if I'd hit paydirt.

I shined my flashlight inside the cab of the truck, but saw no signs of life or unlife inside. The doors were locked. I broke a window using the glass breaker on my combat folder, unlatched the door, and popped the release on the gas cap door. Moving quickly while scanning in both directions, I proceeded to siphon what was left in the tank into my gas cans, and was rewarded with a nearly full can of gas for my efforts. I tossed the empty and the full can in the back of the truck, and then I was on my way.

By this time the sun was peaking over the horizon and I could see the destruction that the pressure wave had created, even this far north of town. Almost every home and building had broken windows, and debris was scattered everywhere. There were a lot more stalled cars in the road, and of course I was also treated to the odd violent vignette, each of which told the tale of some unlucky person or persons who were less than ready for the zombie apocalypse.

As I drove and scanned the roadside for any sign of the motorhome, I wondered whether things were this bad in other parts of the world. It seemed like an awful crazy coincidence to have this plague, or whatever it was, hit us so soon after the bombs dropped. I had to wonder at whether or not it was a bioweapon, as I'd originally speculated, or if it was something... other. That thing that had once been Hillis' son had suggested there was something supernatural or otherworldly behind this mess. I found it hard to accept, but I wasn't going to rule it out, either.

Those were questions for later, after I got my parents safely back to the ranch. I put them out of my mind and continued my slow, careful search for any sign of my folks.

———

As I LEFT Cedar Park behind in the grey dawn of another zombie apocalypse morning, I couldn't help but recall all the times my dad and I had driven this road on our way out to the ranch. Hunting trips at grandpa's place had been a fall ritual around our house. When dove and deer season came around, it had been time to load up the truck on the weekends and head out to the ranch. All my best childhood memories revolved around those trips and our land.

Now, I doubted if I'd ever be able to share those experiences with my own children.

Perhaps someday this would all blow over; maybe the government would find a cure for the plague or whatever was causing the dead to rise, and maybe things would return to normal again, or something close to it. That's what I wanted to hope. But I couldn't help but to replay Corporal Hillis' words in my head, over and over again.

"You think that the government is going to swoop in and

save you? You have no idea how bad things are for your species right now, or what's to come... You are now nothing more than cattle, purposely left alive so we can slaughter you at our leisure."

Fact was, I had no idea if those words had just been the ravings of a sick person or the mad prophecy of something from beyond our world. I couldn't tell if I was going crazy or not myself, but after all I'd been witness to I was starting to lean toward the mad prophecy option.

Damned if I'd be cattle. I'd die with my boots on and my guns blazing, and take as many of those creatures to hell with me on the way. *Cattle, my ass.*

I realized I'd gotten distracted from watching the road. So when I rounded the turn and saw the roadblock, I got a little bit closer to it than I probably would've liked. There were a couple of tractor trailers pulled across the highway, right as you enter what might be called downtown Jonestown. Jonestown had once been known as a haven for meth labs and kitchen chemists, but it had somehow transformed itself into a fairly respectable community in recent years.

But despite the changes that'd been made in the demographic makeup of the community in recent years, I didn't think anyone had bothered to inform the folks who stood on top of the road block. I saw a group of five on top of the trailers and more off to the sides, each of whom could have easily been an extra in a *Sons of Anarchy* spin-off. I noticed a lot of ink, some one-percenter patches, and enough hardware to give the Terminator pause.

None of them drew down on me, but I wasn't going to

risk a confrontation, and especially not with those odds. I pulled a three-point turn and headed back to find a way around the roadblock. As I did, I saw something that caught my eye in the rearview... what looked like the top of a white Winnebago, just on the other side the roadblock.

I stopped in the road for a second, tapping my fingers on the steering wheel and arguing with myself over running their roadblock. I decided that was a dumb idea when one of them started sighting in on me with a high-powered rifle. I floored it and waited until I rounded a curve and was out of their line of sight before I took a left on one of the side streets and parked to weigh my options.

The chances that they'd blocked off the whole town were few and far between. My guess was that they had a few blocks of town barricaded along the main drag, in order to control the most important resources; namely food, fuel, and booze. If that were so, it meant I could probably find a house to hole up in until dark, then go reconnoiter their setup and find some intel on whether or not my folks were in there.

Or, I could just walk up and ask. Real nice. I'm sure that would turn out swell. Nope, I'd take my chances with doing a sneak and peek after dark tonight. It was killing me to have to wait, but I didn't want to take any chances—not with my parents potentially being so close.

I drove out to the edge of town and found an abandoned house with a garage where I could hide the truck. There were a few shamblers roaming around, but none inside the house. I decided to lock everything down so I could get some sleep. I set up some makeshift noise alarms on all the doors, set the alarm on my watch to wake me at dusk, and crashed out with my rifle cradled in my arms across my chest.

———

LATER THAT EVENING, I took off on foot to do some recon of the area behind the roadblock. I packed light so I could move fast if necessary, and soon had eyes on their compound, such as it was. From the looks of it, they used a combination of metal shipping containers, cars and trucks that had been flipped up on their sides, and chain link fence to secure a roughly two block area.

Whoever these guys were, they were organized, because you didn't just fart and build a perimeter like that in a few days. I saw a few people milling around inside the compound, and I could hear genny running in the background too. They had spotlights set up around the place that gave just enough to light to see inside the compound and outside the wall. Every now and again a sentry would shoot a shambler who came too close.

The wall sentries appeared to be using .22 rifles to take out the deaders. I wasn't sure, but it appeared that they used either subsonic ammo, or they had silenced their rifles. Smart. So, the person in charge wasn't your average everyday clown. Good to know.

I needed to get inside that compound; or, at least, I needed to get some intel from someone inside. There were sentries on all the buildings, but they didn't have night vision, and I knew they couldn't watch every quadrant at once. I'd just sit and watch them, and wait until I saw an opportunity to enter the compound and find out what happened to my mom and dad.

Before long, I saw my opening. I noticed that there was a fenced in area behind a restaurant, probably where they had stored their trash cans and whatnot. I also noticed that every so often someone would come out the back door of the place and relieve themselves through the fence, probably so they didn't waste water flushing the toilets unnecessarily inside. After watching a few of them come outside to piss, I made a snap decision and jumped the fence.

Sure enough, within the hour someone walked outside to take a leak. I hid behind the door as it opened, and then snuck up behind the guy and choked him out before he knew what hit him. He smelled like booze and body odor, which was probably better than I smelled at the moment, all things considered. Thankfully, he was a small guy, so after I figured out how to unlock the gate, I had little trouble carrying him a ways off so I could duct tape his mouth and zip-tie him up without being disturbed.

I hoofed it back to the house where I had my truck stowed, only needing to stop once on the way to choke him out again.

Once back at the house, I zip-tied him to a kitchen chair and waited in the dark for him to come around. Sometimes when you choke someone out they regain consciousness right away, but if there's alcohol involved they can be out for several minutes. Finally, I got tired of waiting and ended up slapping him around a bit until he came to.

"Huh... whah?" the guy mumbled as he slowly came around. As his eyes fluttered open, he took stock of his situation quickly and I saw his shoulders slump. "Aw hell. Get that light out of my eyes, will ya? It's giving me a headache. Shit."

Well, this was different. Apparently either this guy was used to being abducted and tied up, or he had balls the size of bowling balls. I continued to shine the light in his face and looked him over. He was about 5'9", give or take, skinny in a rangy sort of way, with long dirty blonde hair and a mustache and beard that would give Gandalf a run for his money. He sort of shrugged and slumped down in the chair under my gaze.

"You wouldn't happen to have any smokes on you, would you?"

I considered playing good cop and giving him one from the stash I got back in Ingram, but decided against it. "I don't smoke."

"Figures." He leaned back in the chair as much as he was able, and squinted at the light. "So, you going to tell me why I'm tied to this chair, or are you going to beat on me a while first?"

"Tell me about the people in the Winnebago."

He tilted his head and smirked. "What, that old couple? They're around. Pulled in yesterday, and Crank convinced them that they were better off staying with us instead of risking the road. Old man said he'd only stay the night, something about meeting his son." He paused, and nodded at me. "I take it you're him."

"Guessed it in one."

He nodded. "Look, man, no harm has come to them, at least not by us. Shit, we were trying to help them..."

I lunged forward and grabbed him by his shirt and jacket, lifting him and the chair off the ground. "What do you mean, 'not by us'?"

His eyes widened for a split second, but that was the only indication he gave that he was rattled. "Settle down, man, settle down! We didn't do nuthin' to them. The old man got hurt last night when we were attacked. He was playing hero, trying to save Crank's kid. Your old man is tough, I'll give him that."

I set him down again, then stepped back to listen. He craned his head at an awkward angle and rubbed his face against his jacket. Coughing, he continued. "Some weird ass shit, let me tell you. This thing came over the walls, moving fast, real fast. Not one of those slow ones—this thing could move, and it was just attacking people all helter-skelter. It went after Crank's kid, and your old man jumped it. He got bit by it, and he hasn't been right since. So Crank put him and your mom up in his own room, and he's been bringing them medicine and shit, doing what he can to make sure the old guy makes it."

I set the flashlight down on the kitchen table so it would illuminate the whole room, then pulled out another chair and sat down. "What's your name?"

He gave me a good long look, and nodded. "Possum, they call me Possum—without an 'O.' On account of how I can hang anywhere, with anyone. No matter how crazy shit gets."

I sighed and ran my hands over my head and face. "Can you take me to them?"

"Yeah, but not like this." He shrugged, as if to indicate his current state of helplessness.

I crossed my arms and thought it over. "Can I trust you, Possum?"

He laughed. "Well, normally if you pulled something like this on one of us, we'd have to kick your ass, maybe break a few bones for the insult. But seeing as how we're in the middle of a zombie apocalypse, I figure we should chalk it up to a misunderstanding. Plus, Crank promised to help your parents find you, once your dad got better. Wouldn't be cool if I had you killed, not after Crank gave his word."

I cut the zip ties on his legs, and then I cut his hands loose. "Just don't try to run. I'm too tired to chase anyone; it's been a long week."

"For everyone, man, for everyone." He rubbed his wrists and stood up.

"I'm Aidan, by the way."

He gave a short nod. "I know. Now c'mon, let's get you over to see your parents."

Possum was smart enough to move quietly and not get chatty on our way back to the compound his MC had cobbled together. As we walked up on their perimeter, he told me to put away my guns so I wouldn't get shot. I obliged him, but made sure I was a few steps behind him as we approached the limit of their spotlights.

Possum called out to the guys standing watch. "Don't shoot! It's me, Possum, and I'm bringing somebody in with me."

I could see the silhouette of someone pointing a rifle at us from on top of the gas station. "Who you bringing with you? Is it a chick?"

"No you doofus, it's Mr. and Mrs. Sullivan's son. I found him earlier tonight. Well, he found me— the point is. he's coming inside with me, and he wants to see his parents."

"Alright, alright, I'll drop the ladder for you." Within a few seconds they'd dropped a 12-foot aluminum ladder down the side of the building, and we were soon scrambling up it to avoid the shamblers who had heard Possum and the sentries yelling back and forth.

A tall biker in a faded and creased leather jacket and a Jolly Roger bandana gave me a hand as I topped the ladder. He turned and slapped Possum on the shoulder. "Hey, how'd you get outside the wall? You know Crank doesn't want anyone roaming around at night."

Possum waved his question off. "It's a long story, man. Anyway, this is Aidan. I'm going to take him to see Crank real quick, then he needs to see his folks."

"Alright. Should I tell Crank you were outside the wall, or not?"

Possum shrugged. "He's going to know in a few minutes anyway. Don't worry about it." At that, Possum motioned for me to follow, and we headed for the other side of the roof, climbing down another ladder to enter the compound.

As we walked, he gestured at various points of interest inside the walls. "We were heading back from a charity ride and stopped here to eat and have a few beers. That's when shit went sideways. It was chaos at first, but Crank calmed folks down and told everyone to stay put. Once the dead people started showing up, that's when things got weird." I gave him a look and he shrugged. "Yeah, I know—no shit. Cops were nowhere to be seen, so Crank got people organized, we killed the goons, and then we got this perimeter set up."

"How many of you guys are ex-military?"

"Crank and a few others. Not me—my dad was military

and we never got along." He pointed off to the northeast. "Anyway, we was going to hole up at the firehouse, but Crank said we needed resources. So, we found some heavy equipment and started barricading ourselves in. Lost a few guys at first though. Had no idea those things were attracted to sound. After that, we started setting up snipers on the buildings, which gave us time until we got the walls up."

I looked around in awe. "How long did it take you guys to do all this?"

He shrugged. "Couple of days. We really just finished it up yesterday. That was when your dad got hurt. C'mon, let me introduce you to Crank."

He walked inside the restaurant and I followed him in. Once inside, I could see that the booths and tables had been used to turn the place into a makeshift barracks. Possum led me through a sea of sleeping bodies and down a back hallway, where he stopped and knocked on a door, Within moments it was opened by a giant of a man. He had to be 6'6" or so, with broad shoulders and hands the size of boxing gloves. He had a grizzled salt and pepper beard, a scar above his left eye, and a look that said he didn't take shit from anyone.

The guy took one look at me and Possum, nodded, and said, "Give me a minute." He turned back into the room and I could hear him talking to someone inside. "No, it's okay, the monsters aren't going to hurt you. Go back to sleep, baby bear. Daddy just has to talk to Possum and then I'll be right back."

He popped back out of the room a moment later with an apologetic look on his face. "Sorry about that. He's been having nightmares since those things first showed up." He tilted his head at me. "Who's this?"

Possum cleared his throat. "He's, um, he's Mr. and Mrs. Sullivan's kid. He, uh, he found me earlier and I promised to take him to his folks."

Crank crossed his arms and wiped his nose with one hand. "He snagged you while you were taking a piss outside." He said it as a statement, not as a question.

Possum looked him in the eye and nodded. Crank shook his head. "Well, no harm done. I can see he left you in one piece. The guys told me you'd snuck over the fence and didn't come back, so I figured you were out looking for a piece of ass to rescue or something." He extended his hand, and I shook it. "I'm Crank. I owe your dad a hell of a debt. If he hadn't acted when he did, I'd have lost my boy."

"Sounds like my dad." I noticed that Crank's hand practically engulfed mine, but despite the iron in his grip there was no challenge there, only respect. "As I understand it, he's been injured. I'd like to see him right away."

Crank and Possum gave each other a knowing look. Crank cleared his throat and screwed up his face in consternation. "Well, it's a little bit worse than that. It's sort of hard to describe, so I'll let you see for yourself. All I can say is, be prepared for a shock, and I'm really sorry." Then, he motioned to us both, and we followed him back outside and next door to an auto repair shop.

I noticed a biker standing guard at the front desk. I gestured at him. "Is that for their protection, or are they being held prisoner?"

Possum responded to my question while Crank just gave me a sad look. "Ain't nobody here a prisoner. Paco there is here to keep an eye on your mom, and help her if she needs anything." We stopped as Crank and Possum pulled up short outside a door that said "Office." They stepped aside and Crank nodded at the door.

"They're inside. I set them up as comfortable as possible. We'll wait out here—well, until you come out."

I could tell by the looks they were giving me that this wasn't going to be good. So, I steeled myself for the worst and stepped through the door.

———

As I walked in, I noticed that the desk had been removed and a bed had been set up against the far wall. Someone was sleeping fitfully in it, covered in blankets and facing away from the door. There was a recliner in the corner, a side table, and a battery-operated camping lantern. I saw a few cases of bottled water and some food stacked up on the floor, and a loaded revolver on the side table next to the lantern. My mother was sitting in the recliner, reading the Bible by the light of the lantern. She looked up as I entered, and as she recognized me I could see her tearing up.

"Oh, *mijo*—I knew you'd find us." She stood up and met me at the center of the small room, and I gave her a big hug.

I tried not to cry. "I found the note you left me, Mama. But I had to kill Mr. Keller from across the street." I made the admission like a child who was admitting to breaking a window. All the emotion I'd been holding in over the past week came flooding back in a rush, and tears began to fall from my eyes.

She leaned back and wiped my cheeks with her thumbs. "I'm sure you did him a favor, *mijo*. Now he can be at peace." She glanced over at the bed. "I only wish I could say the same for your father, though."

I sucked it up and wiped my eyes dry. "What's wrong with him? The guys who brought me in here said he got bit by one of those creatures."

She nodded sagely. "They may look rough, but they're good boys. They've been looking after us. Sometimes he recognizes me, other times he doesn't. He's very ill, Aidan."

At that I heard what could only be described as a growl coming from the bed. There was the clink of metal on metal, and as my father stirred the covers fell away to reveal that he'd been handcuffed to the bed. These were not the strong and gentle hands that'd held me when I had nightmares, that had bandaged my cuts and bruises, that had greeted me with a handshake and a hug when I'd returned from Afghanistan. Aghast, I walked over to the bed and pulled the covers back, and what I saw then will haunt me for the rest of my days.

It was my dad, that much was for certain, but his body was in the process of transforming into something... other. His fingers were elongating slightly, and the nails were lengthening. His skin was pale and yellowed, and his hair was beginning to fall out in strands and clumps. As I leaned over him to get a better look, his eyes popped open, and I noticed immediately that they were no longer human. He growled at me briefly, and then he blinked. I was too stunned to react, so I just stood there, looking at him in awe and grief.

His eyelids fluttered, and I saw some recognition creep into his eyes. "Aidan—Aidan, is that you?"

I grabbed his hand, forcing myself not to recoil at the rough, cold, clammy feel of his skin. "Yeah, Dad, it's me. I finally found you and Mom."

He smiled, and I could see that his gums were bleeding. He was missing a few teeth, and there were small, sharp, white points poking out from his bloody gums where those teeth had once been. "That's good, son, I'm proud of you." His voice was raspy and soft, but I could hear his familiar baritone as he squeezed my hand and pulled me closer.

"Son, you know what you have to do. Your mother—she doesn't have the courage to do it. She was never a soldier, never had to make the choices we've had to make." Although his eyes were clear, his expression was frantic. "I saw that thing that did this to me, and I know what I'm going to become. You have to kill me, before I end up like that. Promise me, son—promise me you'll do it before I hurt someone."

I wept, and tears streamed off my face to land on his as I replied. "I promise, Dad. I won't let you down."

He relaxed visibly at those words, and he patted my hand before he released it. "That's good, son. You've made me proud, every single day of your life. You should know that. Your grandfather always said that you were the best of us. Now, let me spend some time alone with your mother, while I'm able."

"I love you, Pops." I leaned over and kissed him on the forehead.

"I know, son."

As I turned away, my mom took my place at his side. She cried too. I placed a hand on her shoulder. "I'll be right outside, Mom. Just come get me when you're ready." She nodded and sat astride the bed next to my father, and I stopped to take one last look at them as a couple before I walked out the door.

I wiped my eyes, noting that Crank and Possum looked away in order to give me the dignity that the moment deserved. After I'd composed myself, Crank walked up and placed a firm hand on my shoulder. He looked me in the eye and smiled.

"Your dad, he's a great man. I wish I would have had a dad like that. I owe him a debt I'll never be able to repay. Never."

I nodded. "The greatest man I'll ever know."

Possum spoke up as Crank stepped back to give me some breathing room. "Hey Aidan, are you hungry? We can get you some grub—"

BANG! The shot rang out from inside the room, and we all reacted at once, rushing into the room in single file, almost as if we were stacked up to do a room entry. As we burst in, I saw the revolver dangling from my mother's hand, and the sharp tang of burning gunpowder hit my nose. My father had a perfect small hole in the middle of his forehead, and a peaceful look on his face. His eyes were closed, and if I didn't know better I might have thought he slept.

I sprang forward and gently took the gun from my mother, then I held her tight. "Mama, why didn't you let me take care of him? I promised him I would."

"I know, son. But there's no way I was going to let you live the rest of your life with that on your conscience. He was my constant companion for thirty-five years, and I was his. It was my responsibility to see to his last wishes, not yours. Now it's my burden to bear."

I rocked slowly back and forth as I held her close. Soon, she pushed me away, gently, and looked up at me with resignation in her eyes. "I'd like to take your father home now, Aidan."

I nodded. Crank spoke from somewhere near the door. "Aidan, Mrs. Sullivan—me and the boys will help you take care of his body. You won't need to do a thing."

My mother turned and patted him on the arm. "Thank you, Darnell." Apparently, my mom had already been playing mother to these guys. Such a charmer, she was. I bet no one else called Crank by his real name, except maybe his own mother.

We stood by as Crank, Possum, and a few of his guys carefully wrapped the body up and prepared it for transporting back to the ranch. Then, I went back to the house where I had holed up, retrieved the truck, and we loaded Dad up and headed back to the ranch.

———

WE GOT BACK to the ranch without incident. I knew what to look for and what to avoid now, and I was able to steer us clear of much of the trouble I'd run into on my way to Austin days before. I felt guilty about not stopping to check in on Rayden, Elena, and Bibi, but I wanted to get back to the ranch and get my mom settled in as soon as possible. I told myself I'd check on them just as soon as I got Dad buried and Mom was okay.

It was nice and sunny when we got back, and I wasted no time in getting Dad buried on the land he loved so much. We buried him out behind the cabin; Mom said he had always liked the trees back there. I said a prayer over his grave, and Mom read some Scripture. Afterward, we stood there in silence for a good long time, and then Mom grabbed my hand and led me back inside the house.

I offered to make her something to eat, but she declined. "No, I'm tired, son. I think I'm going to go lay down for a while."

"Alright, Mom. I'll come in and check on you before I go to bed." I kissed her on the forehead, and she returned the favor with a peck on my cheek.

"Your father was very proud of you Aidan—you were his pride and joy. Never forget that."

"I won't, Mama. Now, go get some rest." She smiled and retired to the bedroom, and as I watched her go my heart sank at what she had had to do for my dad. I took some small satisfaction in the fact that he would be at peace now, but not much.

Later that evening I went in to check on her, but she had

fallen fast asleep so I let her rest. I drifted off that night to the sound of cicadas and static from the weather radio. My last thoughts before falling asleep were not of revenge necessarily, but concern about all the people out there who were left, the people who couldn't defend themselves against these new threats.

I slept fitfully that night, my dreams filled with nightmares of my dad coming to drain the blood from my mother. In my dreams, I could only look on, frozen in terror and grief as I watched my mother perish at my father's hands. Her eyes stared at me imploringly as he drank, but no sound arose from her lips, save small infrequent gurgles as I watched her drowning in her own blood, time and time again.

EPILOGUE

My mother died that night in her sleep; I suppose that the strain of having to take my father's life had just been too much for her. I buried her out back next to my dad, and wasted little time afterward preparing for what I knew I had to do. I drove all day to get back to Crank and his people in Jonestown. There'd been another attack the night before in my absence, and Possum had been killed defending a mother and her kids.

Crank and I tracked down the thing that had killed Dad and Possum, which ironically led us only a few houses down from the house where I'd holed up. We set the house on fire, and when the thing came screaming out of an upstairs window I put two rounds in its head, and Crank blew off its leg with a sawed off 12 gauge. I walked up on it as it rolled around on the ground—a charred, smoldering, bloody heap—and placed several more rounds in its skull until it stopped moving.

I carved a Roman numeral two on its chest and tied it up with barbed wire near their road block, spit Vlad the Impaler style on a pole that once held a speed limit sign. When he saw what I'd done, Crank whistled in shock and horror at my work.

I responded without taking my eyes from the vamp. "Don't worry, I'm not going crazy—least not any more so than I already am. This is just a warning, in case any more of those things come around your place. Hopefully it'll make 'em think twice about settling in these parts."

He nodded once and walked off. I guess psy ops just wasn't his thing.

———

THE NEXT DAY I headed back to Fredericksburg and found Bibi, Elena, and Rayden still at the same little cottage I'd left them at days before. Bibi filled me in on what had happened at the high school, and as it turned out folks hadn't taken too kindly to Captain Hillis selling them out. A few of his men stayed loyal, but the rest turned on him and summarily executed him and all the soldiers and cops who were in on it.

Only a few of the cops had known what was going on. Currently they were in the process of setting up a provisional government and making sure that nothing like that could happen again. Bibi said she was fine right where she was, but I wasn't so sure. I helped her and the kids get settled into a more defensible home, one with more space as well, and spent several days running back and forth from the local hardware store with supplies to make it zombie-proof.

It still wouldn't keep out one of those nosferatu-looking things, but at least they'd be safe if some shamblers got through the fence. Rayden, true to form, had scavenged a supply of weapons and ammo from local homes and stores, and I spent a considerable amount of time showing him how to maintain and operate every single one. We also spent time on marksmanship, and by the time I left them I was certain he was prepared to defend Bibi and Elena. He would turn out to be a good man, someday. Heck, he was already most of the way there.

I eventually tracked down Dan, Sarah, and their kids at her parents' place near Rock Springs. They were doing fine, and Buttercup eventually had a litter of half-Catahoula, half-Bulldog pups. They offered me pick of the litter, but I declined. I was too busy with work to raise a pup, but I told them I might come back for one when they got a little older.

These days I spend most of my time helping folks, doing what I do best. Not everybody is cut out to handle these creatures, so I spend my time searching for settlements and communities that have sprouted up out here, and taking care of the creatures they can't take care of themselves. It doesn't pay much, and mostly people pay me in barter if at all, but I don't do it for that.

Nope. I do it for the chance to scratch one more number on the chest of one of those things, and to string up one more corpse to warn these hell-swine that we Texans don't take shit lying down. So far, I'm up to a dozen since the one I killed in

Jonestown. Thirteen total; maybe there's some symbolism there, if you believe in that crap.

———

Folks call me Scratch. And if you're one of Them and we cross paths, chances are good I'm going to send you back where you came from and mount your carcass up as a trophy and warning both...

Listen, you might *think* you're superior to us, and that we're just cattle who only exist for your sick amusement. But honestly, I don't care what you think. There's only one thing you need to know about me, and it's this—

Because of me, your days on this earth are numbered. You can count on it.

NEWSLETTER

This concludes Invasion: Zombie Apocalypse... But the story continues in Incursion: Vampire Apocalypse! Look for it at all major online booksellers.

Also, be sure to sign up for my newsletter at http://MDMassey.com for your FREE ebook!

M.D. Massey has been a soldier, an emergency room techni-
cian, a fitness trainer, a truck driver, a martial arts instructor,
a cook, a consultant, a web designer, and a security profes-
sional. He also spent six weeks in law school before deciding
that, if he was going to lie for a living, he'd do it honestly as a
fiction writer. M.D. lives in Austin, Texas with his family and
a huge American Bulldog who keeps him company while he
writes the sort of books he likes to read.

Find out more and get your FREE book at:
http://MDMassey.com

91769944R00105